THE MERCY SISTERS
LOVE KNOCKED

J. NICHOLE

not the last page

To all those who love and appreciate Black Love, this is for us!

J. NICHOLE NEWSLETTER

I'd love to keep in touch with you, and if you feel the same, join my newsletter.

By the way, for joining, I'll send you a free book!
https://mailchi.mp/notthelastpage/ebook

CHAPTER ONE

MARCIA

"What about this one?" I asked, moving around to show my sisters all my angles. "Makes my ass look just right, right?" Nic looked away from the screen and coughed, and Liv's eyes widened as she stared straight at me. "What?" My sisters weren't ever quiet on their opinion. I was expecting them to either tell me they hated it, or loved it, but silence, not their M.O. at all.

"If you like it"—Liv shrugged—"I love it."

I sighed then offered, "I don't want you to just like it because I like it." I thought about my thirtieth birthday and all I wanted it to be. "You know I'm turning thirty."

Nic shook her head. "We know, Marcia, we know." I was sensing some irritation in her voice. "Hell, the whole town knows." She was squinting into the phone. "In fact"—she nodded her head—"grab sis, over there." She pointed at the phone and I looked behind me. "I bet she even knows about your birthday party this weekend."

Liv joined in with Nic laughing. I rolled my eyes and said, "She should know, this town is not that big." I smirked. "I want everyone to know."

Rolling Hills was not extremely small, but it did have that small town vibe. It was like I knew just about everyone, and the folks I didn't know, they likely knew of me or one of my sisters.

I returned to the clothes rack, with my sisters still on the screen as I looked at a few of the other dresses. As I scanned, I casually asked, "Do either of you have a date yet?" To which each of them scoffed.

"The important question is..." Liv cocked her head. "Do you have a date?" When I shook my head, she laughed and replied, "You know Mom has been threatening to send a man our way if we are still single by thirty."

"Oh, I know," I responded. Our mother, bless her heart, was determined to have each of her girls married off with children, even if it took an arranged marriage to get it accomplished. I was the first to hit the thirty-year mark, so neither of us knew if she was just joking or would actually try to make it happen. "Do you think she'd really?" Then before I could even finish, they were both agreeing in unison. "Right." Our mom wasn't the joking type; she was all business, all the time.

"I mean..." Liv shrugged. "Who is left in Rolling Hills? Between the three of us, we've likely dated every eligible bachelor there is here." Then she laughed. "Maybe she'll import a guy in for us."

"Can you just imagine Marcia saying, 'I like whatever you like'?" We all laughed, then I found a dress and shrieked. "If we shall be having a man from a foreign land, a prince of sorts, I'm going to need you not to shriek in public."

"I found the perfect dress." I didn't need either of their opinions raining on my parade, though, so I told them, "Just wait till you see it on me this weekend." Then I went back to my other dilemma. "And how about we kick the weekend off early, meet me for drinks tonight." I grinned. "Maybe, we'll find a few guys we can bring to the party."

Liv replied with a 'hell yeah,' but Nic was slow to respond. "But I—" Before she could give us a lame excuse, we told her to get dressed and down to our favorite bar.

I tried on the red dress, and as I hoped, it was snug where it needed to be snug, and popping where it needed to pop. When I placed it on the counter, the sales clerk smiled and said, "This is perfect for your party," as if I had been talking to her about it. "Sorry, I didn't mean to eavesdrop, but I heard you on the phone." I laughed, and then apologized for being loud. "Not like we have a ton of customers." The boutique was unusually empty.

I looked over my shoulder and around the store, then asked, "What's up with that anyway?" I knew the place was a little pricey, which was the reason I loved shopping there. It was exclusive.

She gritted her teeth then announced softly, "A little competition across town." I narrowed my eyes. "The boutique on Ellis Street."

I felt bad for being excited when I asked, "Oh. It's open now?" She nodded her head, then I reassured her, "Don't worry about me, I love coming here."

"In that case, I can't wait to see you next time." She handed me my bag and added, "And I hope your prince will be everything you desire." She winked.

By the time I made it to Sweet Vine, my sisters already had a bottle of wine at the table and a glass poured for me. I sat down across from Liv, and said, "Thank you," with a sigh before I took a decent-size sip. "You know this is my favorite." I smiled when I looked beside me to Nic.

Nic raised her glass in the air and announced, "To us finding some quality peen tonight." Both she and Liv cackled, and I upturned my nose. "Oh, what? You aren't looking for the peen?" I shook my head. "I thought that was the reason we were meeting you here."

My nose was still scrunched when I told her, "I'm out here waiting for Mr. Wonderful to roll up on me. I'm not here looking for just somebody I can fuck for the night."

Liv raised her glass in the air again, and without me or Nic joining her, she said, "To *Marcia* finding *Mr. Everything.*" She nodded her head, satisfied with herself. I started to reject the idea that the guy I wanted had to be everything, but then I considered my expectations, and well, yeah, he needed to be everything. "Okay..." Liv's head was on a swivel before it stopped in the direction of a group of guys near the bar. "Him." She cocked her head and my eyes followed, but I had no idea which him she was pointing out. "The one with the blue suit jacket."

Nic quickly interrupted, "Not him." And she didn't even need to elaborate. Being close in age, it wasn't totally out of the ordinary for one of us to bump into a guy another one of us had dated. We usually give each other a fair warning—shared our random encounters with guys—and certainly made sure we each knew which guy was off limits. Nic's burgundy-painted lip curled up. "He talks way too damn much."

"Are you serious right now?" Liv shifted in her seat. "Did you forget we live in Rolling Hills? Population of maybe twenty thousand people, and of that even less available, *potential,* black men." Liv took a large gulp of her wine. "Do we have room to be worried about a guy talking too much?"

Nic and I both nodded our heads. "Absolutely," I said honestly. "Just because we have a small pool of available guys doesn't mean I should lower my standards, right?" I looked at her over the rim of my wine glass. "Besides, who says our guy has to be from Rolling Hills?" Each of us had left for college and returned home, but being away wasn't foreign—no matter how much my mom tried to convince us we had to be in Rolling Hills to help with the family business.

And Liv reminded us of that when she said, "Oh, and Mama

is going to be okay with us up and leaving?" She cocked her head and the smirk on her face reminded me of when she was a kid and wasn't getting her way.

I shrugged. "I mean, yeah."

Then Nic chimed in, "Anyway, tonight, it's about the peen. Let's see what we can find." As if on cue, a couple of guys walked over to the table, one being the guy Nic claimed talked too much.

"Hey." A tall guy with dark skin, a pretty smile, but in dire need of a haircut sat beside me. "Mind if we join you?"

I shook my head as the other guys were cozying up to my sisters. Liv ended up next to the guy who talked too much, and her eyes widened as he sat beside her and immediately started asking her questions. "Are you from here?" I asked, knowing I hadn't seen them before.

The guy sitting beside me, Curtis, said, "He is," looking at Liv's guy. "We're family, just in town for the weekend." I tried to conceal my grin, because he wasn't from Rolling Hills, and maybe, just maybe, he had potential. "Are you all from here?" he asked, and as he spoke I tried to pick up on his accent, but failed miserably. I nodded my head. "Wait, are you all sisters?"

I nodded again. "We are." We didn't think we favored each other. Besides our dark skin, and maybe the shape of our eyes, we each had varying features. Each of us argued who favored either of our parents more. "Most people assume cousins, but we are indeed sisters."

Curtis looked to each of my sisters, briefly, then back to me. "Tell me, what'd you all do in this city growing up?"

"What most kids do." I narrowed my eyes. "I guess? We hung out with friends most of the time." Then I beamed, "Having sisters around the same age was cool. For a while, we just hung out with each other."

"I guess that's cool." He pointed to his people and said, "We hung out together most of the time, and I could only imagine if we lived in the same house."

I was kinda feeling Curtis—laughing at his little jokes, letting my hand brush up against his knee. We even danced and I let my ass back up on him. The music changed up to a slow R&B song, and we were close enough to share a breath.

We sat back at the table, but Liv and Nic didn't look like they were enjoying themselves as much as I was, so I asked if they wanted to hit the bathroom. It was there when Liv confirmed, "Damn, I didn't think any one person could talk that much." She cringed. "My ears hurt."

We laughed, but then Nic added, "And his cousin, *Dante*, thinks he is God's gift to women. I thought I liked a confident man, but damn." She shook her head. Then they both stopped, and Nic laughed. "But you, ma'am." She stared at me. "You seem to have lucked up tonight."

I hesitated but then said, "Maybe so?" Then I started to brag on Curtis a little bit. "I mean, he seems to be a decent dude." I gritted my teeth. "His haircut could use some work, but..." I waved my hand in the air. "That can be fixed. He has a cool personality, easy to talk to, and he can dance."

"And you know what that means." Nic's smile was beaming, but I shook my head. "That he can fuck," she said matter-of-factly, and I shook my head some more, but Liv, little Liv, was agreeing with her.

"Okay, but if you all are ready to go, I can grab his number and catch up with him later." I scrunched my nose. "I don't want to make you suffer on my behalf."

Neither of them was going for that. "But it's your birthday weekend, and maybe this is your guy." Liv placed a hand on my shoulder and ushered me out of the bathroom. "Gotta give it a shot."

The guys were laughing when we made it back to the table

and took our seats. "What are you laughing at?" I asked.

"Dante was just saying maybe I found my new home." Curtis looked past me to where Dante was sitting. But my face twisted in response.

"Your new home?" I asked, and he nodded his head. "And what happened to your old home?"

He laughed and then replied, "Well," he cleared his throat before he continued, "I'm kinda in between jobs right now, and looking for a new place to live." He may have said more, or not, but he lost me at *in between jobs.*

Liv must've noticed my face, because she chipped in when I couldn't find any words to respond. "So, what is it you do exactly?"

I tuned back into that response, because maybe he had it like that, where he could just be floating around looking for work. He didn't look at me when he said, "I do whatever, I'm not picky." The air left out of my lungs, and the gasping sound I made was likely louder than the song playing over the speakers.

Nic tried to cover for me, but her response didn't do much to help me recover. I tapped his knee and said, "It's getting a little late, and I do have to go to work in the morning. I should get going." That didn't seem to rattle him much. He still leaned into my ear and asked for my phone number. "Ugh, yeah, so I don't think that's a good idea," I admitted before standing to walk away.

As soon as I felt the fresh air on my skin, I laughed, uncontrollably. "Did that grown ass man just say he does *whatever?*"

"But then he added, 'he's not picky,'" Liv said, followed by more laughter.

"Told you we should have just stuck with the mission to find peen. At least you'd be thoroughly fucked instead of thoroughly disappointed at the end of the night." I rolled my eyes and walked to my car, leaving the two of them behind bent over in laughter.

CHAPTER TWO

Joseph

With a wrench in hand, I yelled, "I think that's it," to Alonzo, who was down the hall in the bathroom. When I heard the water running, but didn't see a leak coming from the kitchen sink, I sighed in relief. "It's good."

I wiped my hands on my pants and stood from the floor. Mrs. Porter walked into the kitchen with her hands clasped together. "Is it fixed?" she whispered. I nodded my head and she nearly jumped from the door into my arms. "Thank you, God."

I had to agree with her. I had seen some wild plumbing situations in my time, but the bathroom causing a kitchen leak was new to me. Alonzo walked into the kitchen with a goofy ass grin on his face. "I knew if I couldn't get it done, you'd figure it out."

I shrugged. "But I do think there's more work to be done here, Mrs. Porter." She frowned. "Not today, and maybe not even in a few months, but eventually we should replace this old piping." Her hand went to her forehead. "We'll get there, Mrs. Porter." I felt bad for dropping that on her. I knew since her husband had passed away she was struggling to keep the house maintained.

But I didn't expect her to walk us out and her hand to dip a little low on my waistline. I turned to her when we got outside, and the grin on her face let me know everything I needed to know.

"Mrs. Porter needs her old piping replaced, alright," Alonzo declared. I tried to ignore him as I climbed into the truck, but he insisted on giving me the details of the situation I was just in. I pulled out of the driveway and Alonzo said, "If it weren't for how hard it was to fix, I'd almost believe she may have broken some shit just to see you."

"I mean, if someone on the team knew how to troubleshoot, I wouldn't even be here." That shut him up most of the ride back to the office.

"Are you saying you wouldn't dip into some of that cougar love?" I looked to my side, and the look on Alonzo's face, looking stoic, no smile, actually made me think he was serious. "Just imagine it." He pointed a finger to his forehead. "She can cook you a nice ass meal, fill you up." I was shaking my head. "Then she probably doesn't even nag, or want much. Hell, her husband left her in a decent spot."

"Remind me not to send you back to Mrs. Porter's house," I said as we pulled into the parking lot of our office. He cocked his head and asked if I really wouldn't consider it, and I replied, "No, man, damn. I mean, I know Rolling Hills is lacking on the available women, but someone my mama's age?" I shook my head even harder. "Hell no." He shrugged, grabbed his tools, and stepped out of the truck.

I walked inside and forgot about what he was saying until my phone rang. "Hello?" I said in a hurry, as I was trying to wrap up for the day.

"Jojo," I could hear my mom shouting like she didn't have the phone right up to her ear. "Can you hear me?" I sighed and told her I heard her very well. "Where are you? I thought you would be here early to prepare for your speech."

"No, Mama, I told you I would not be there early and that I'd be rushing over after work." I locked the office door behind me. "I'm on my way." When she offered to stay on the phone with me, I declined. I didn't need her asking me every other minute how close I was to the spot. "I'll see you in about fifteen minutes," I told her, then hung up.

Since retiring, my mama had become a Rolling Hills socialite, as she liked to be called. But her active lifestyle meant she often volunteered me for random shit. Like the event I was pulling up to, speaking to the young men in the community about getting their lives together.

I straightened my collar, stood tall, and walked into the community center. Many of the young dudes I saw when I walked in were guys I saw in church on Sunday, or on the basketball court in the middle of the week. I casually talked to them, made sure they weren't staying in the streets too late, going to school, and keeping decent grades. Talking to them in a formal setting wouldn't be much different.

Except when I was stopped by the event coordinator, Kiara, she directed me to the stage where three other men sat at a table. "Kiara," I whispered as she showed me to my seat, "I thought I was just speaking for a few minutes?" I narrowed my eyes.

She smiled wide, and said, "You will, don't worry about it, you'll do great," before she scurried off the stage.

I looked out into the audience, growing larger, as the moderator joined us on stage. "Good evening, ladies and gentlemen," the black guy, around my age, greeted the crowd before turning to us and announcing, "Tonight we will have a lively discussion with three successful men, from right here in Rolling Hills."

I found my mama in the sea of people, and although she was beaming, I wanted to tell her she set me up, again.

After our introductions, the moderator started a round of rapid-fire questions, and although the questions weren't tough, I could see the boys looking bored. So when it was my turn up to the mic again, I said, "You know, if we were one of your favorite rappers, or basketball players, favorite actors even, you'd likely be listening to every word we say, so interested in how we got to where we are." I heard a little chatter, some laughter from a few boys in the back of the room. "The level of success you obtain, and who you will be, if you'll be the next LeBron, or Lil' Baby, or a multi-millionaire, all depends on what you do now." I paused, then said, "If you are thinking whatever it is you want to be doesn't look like me," I turned to the guys beside me, each dressed in their Sunday best, "or them, these nuggets we are dropping on you tonight will help you get there. So pay attention, now, in the classroom, at home, don't sit back and think you'll just get there because you want to be there." I could hear the guys beside me agreeing. "It'll take work."

"And with that, I have one last question." The moderator asked us, "What's the one thing you can tell these young men, that you wished someone would have told you?"

I decided to sit back and think about my response as the other two answered. "I'll be honest," I said when it was my turn to speak again, "I wish someone would have told me just how hard it would be to be an adult." I laughed. "It ain't easy."

When I walked off the stage, I had a few moms step to me and thank me for being honest. I even had one of the kids come up and ask, "Man, is it really that hard?" with a smirk on his face.

"You'll find out," is all I replied.

I found my mom on the other side of the room talking to a beautiful older woman, but she walked away before I approached. "Please don't tell me you offered me up for another little event."

She gritted her teeth then said, "Not exactly." I cocked my head and rubbed my hand across my beard. "What would you say if I told you, I have a date for you?"

I shook my head. "I'd say I'm not interested." Since I broke up with my last girlfriend, my mama had been trying to hook me up with some of everybody—her friends' daughters, members of the church, random women she met at the grocery store. "I told you, I'm good," I reminded her. Then her smile disappeared, and those eyes that would make me walk across a field of broken glass appeared, and I sighed, "Okay. Who is it?"

"If you agree, you'll meet her on Saturday." Her smile grew wide, and I knew she got me, again. She said, "I'll send you the details," as if it were some business deal she was managing.

"Wait, what?" I asked, but before I could get her to give me more details, her eyes were set across the room and she was on the move, pulling me behind her.

Announcing, "Wasn't he amazing?" as she flaunted me across the room to different moms. I was starting to feel she had a different agenda that she was keeping from me.

When the night was over, I told her, "I'm starting to feel like you are trying really hard to get me set up." Her face was blank and she didn't respond. "Ma." I looked down at her. "For real?"

She shifted then finally responded, "It's just that you seemed so heartbroken when you and Jessica broke up." I shrugged. "And it's been a while, right?" I hadn't thought about the time much, because I was over it. "I just think it's time my baby was in love again."

"Oh, Mama," I said before wrapping my arms around her. "I have all the love I need right here."

"Yeah, remember that on Saturday, okay?" She laughed and got into her car. "Drive safe, and let me know when you make it home."

CHAPTER THREE

MARCIA

"And you are both going to be here in two, *two*," I had to emphasize, because both Liv and Nic were notorious for being late, "hours to ride with me, right?" They both mumbled, and then I heard a knock at the door.

"Who is at your door?" Nic asked. I laughed as I sauntered across my condo, thinking she and Liv were showing up early.

"Aw, you came early," I said as I started opening the door. "Oh, hi," I said to the man who was standing firm in front of my door—tall, dark, and handsome was always such a cliché phrase until I saw whomever it was standing there in front of me.

Then he opened his mouth, and I expected him to tell me he had a package for me. I quickly looked down to the crease in his pants and a package he had for sure. "Marcia?" he asked, breaking my inappropriate gaze at his lump.

"Yes?" My sisters were still in my ear, but I couldn't understand what they were mumbling because all my attention was on him. The beard that framed his jawline was perfectly manicured, and his fresh cut was noticeable. Then I realized he wasn't in the typical delivery gear—no brown shorts and shirt.

His face crinkled before he put his hand to his head. "I don't even know how to say this." Then I thought he was a neighbor I hadn't met before who needed to borrow something. And the way he was looking, he could have the whole damn canister of sugar.

"Okay?" I said finally, after we both stared at each other for a minute.

"I'm here to take you to your party tonight."

As fine as he was, my response was still the same as my sisters who couldn't even see his deep chocolate skin, beautiful brown eyes, straight, white teeth, and fresh from the barber cut. "What?" My eyes narrowed, and I waited for him to respond.

"Your mom." He shrugged then looked like he was contemplating his next words. "There's no way you need a date." And my mouth dropped. "Shit, that didn't sound right."

"Give me a minute," I said, closing the door in his face.

"Did he just say he was there to take you to your party?" I heard Liv asking.

Then Nic asked the only question that mattered to her, "But what did he look like?" She gasped, "Because if he looks like he sounds, give him my address, and I'll have a private party ready and waiting for him when he gets here." I laughed, briefly.

"He said *our mother* sent him here," I finally blurted out. "Why would our mother, Lisa Mercy, send a man to *my house* to take me to my birthday party?" I paced the floor. "What am I, one of her foundations? A charity case?" I went on and on then heard another knock at the door, and I sighed. "And he's actually standing out there like he expects me to be okay with this."

"I mean," Liv interrupted my banter, "she did say if we didn't have a man by thirty she was sending one our way."

Then we collectively groaned. "Too damn much," I finally said as I walked back to the door. "Let me call you back."

"As much as I believe you are here with good intentions..." I looked at him then quickly away, because the way he licked his lips had me wanting to say fuck the party. "I don't need a date."

His eyes widened then narrowed. "Oh, you have one already?" *This motherfucker.*

I bit my lip. "No, I don't need a date to my birthday party." I shook my head. "Why do you just assume I need a date?" I felt myself wanting to argue with him like he was the problem, when actually it was my mother who needed to hear every word I had to say.

Before I closed the door, he said, "If it's any consolation, my mama can't stay out of my business either." He winked. And if it weren't for the point I had to prove to my own mama, I would have had him all up in and around my party. But it was the principle.

I stood against the back of the door while his smile, and those eyes, were pierced into my memory. I was close to opening the door and at least asking him for his phone number, but I decided against it.

Instead, I walked into the kitchen and opened a bottle of wine, the vintage bottle I bought years ago, for a special occasion. And what could be more special than my thirtieth birthday? I poured up a full glass and clicked through my phone till my mom's picture displayed. I took a few more sips from my glass then dialed her number. "My birthday girl."

"Really, Mama?" I said before she could go any further. "You thought it was a good idea to have some man just show up to my place and take me to my party tonight?"

"Oh," she paused, "he's timely. I like that. Don't you like that? You like to be on time."

"Mama," I took another sip from my glass before I continued, "I'm not a charity case. I don't need your help in my love life. And," she tried to speak but my words kept flowing, "why are you stuck on us being married off by thirty?"

I get it, my mom and dad married young, like their early twenties, so maybe thirty doesn't sound crazy, but still. "Marcia Denise Mercy." My eyes widened. "I don't understand why you and your sisters are dead set on remaining single." She huffed.

"You act like we are out here fighting off an army of men."

"Oh, well then, I'll see the gentleman tonight?" I could imagine her smiling and it made my blood boil. My mama was a true businesswoman; she'd negotiate you down until the terms were favorable for her.

But I wasn't giving in. "Actually, you won't. I declined his offer to join me." I didn't realize I could smile that wide.

"You are insufferable. I'll see you at the party." She hung up the phone before I could say anything else. I looked at the time and remembered I still had to finish getting dressed. I put down my phone, but not my wine glass, and made my way to my bedroom.

The dress I bought at the boutique was stretched out across my bed, accessories beside it, and my shoes on the floor—like I was headed to my first day of high school. In the bathroom I fluffed my coils and applied my makeup, finishing my look with a deep-red lipstick. As I puckered my lips in the mirror, I saw —*damn, what is his name?* My mama had me fantasizing about a man I didn't know shit about. But if she thought he should take me out, he had to be hot shit—like Rolling Hill's most eligible bachelor. Probably a doctor, new to town, some tech-magnate; otherwise, she would not have found him suitable enough for *her daughter*.

I gave up thinking about who he was and what he did, because it was likely I wouldn't see him again. Just as I was stepping into my shoes, I heard another knock at the door. This time, with a lot less bass. "On time?" I raised my brow. "I'm in awe," I said as Liv and Nic pushed past me carrying a bottle of champagne and crystal flutes.

"We know you would have had an entire meltdown if we were late," Nic exclaimed. Then she stopped and looked me up and down before she said, "I approve of this dress. Yes, Marcia." Liv grinned and nodded her head.

I did a little twirl for them for effect. "I'm glad you like it." Then I smirked. "Too bad that man won't be there to see me in this." Then my eyes widened, and I added, "Can you believe I don't even know his name?"

"Yes, because you treated that man like trash." Liv rolled her eyes. "Hopefully, when the universe connects you again you'll be more grateful."

"Yeah, and maybe give him some pussy as a consolation prize," Nic joked as she handed me a flute full with champagne. "To chapter thirty." She winked. "May your best days be ahead of you."

"And may you be open to new possibilities," Liv added.

We stood in front of my expansive windows and took a ton of pictures before I announced, "We better get going before I'm more than fashionably late to my own party."

They both nodded and headed toward the door. "By the way..." Liv smiled. "Mama is overbearing, but she does come through for the event planning, just wait till you see what other surprises she has in store for you today." I followed them outside, and my mouth dropped when I saw a man standing with the door of a Bentley truck wide open.

"The Bentley?" I asked, and Liv nodded. "Damn," I said as we approached the driver. "Maybe I kinda, almost, forgive her for sending that sexy stranger to my door." They both laughed and climbed into the car.

"You know Mama is extra." Nic shrugged. "I'm bracing myself for how this restaurant will be decorated." I smiled because I was there for all the extra—the glitz, the glam, the expensive, the too much. Nic looked at my wide grin and shook her head. "And you are all here for it, right?" I nodded my head.

When the driver pulled up to Cornerstone, I felt like a celebrity. There was a red carpet accompanied by a photographer and a few familiar faces standing outside. "The extra," I said, then added, "give me all of that." I waited for Nic and Liv to step out of the truck and move aside, before I made my entrance. I heard the flashes of the cameras snapping, and the smile on my face didn't falter for a second.

I took my time greeting my friends, some that flew in from random cities around the country. "Thank you for coming," I said as I shook hands. A few of my homegirls had their boos, or even husbands, with them. And for a brief second, I felt a hint of jealousy. That could have been me, maybe if I wasn't in Rolling Hills. Then I saw my mother emerge from the crowd, her arms stretched wide.

"Did you enjoy your ride over?" my mom asked. I nodded my head as I heard my dad mumble, likely not excited about the amount of cash she dropped for my birthday. "Just wait till we get inside," she gushed, as if a few hours ago she hadn't hung up on me.

"Happy birthday, Marci," my dad said, reaching in for a hug.

"Thank you." I kissed his cheek. "For everything." His eyes beamed, and although I'm sure he was in sticker shock, for that moment, all was well.

My mom tugged me by the arm, and I followed her inside where you'd think I was entering my wedding reception. The amount of flowers, and candles, and art decor was overwhelmingly amazing. "Wow," I said, and heard my dad mumbling more behind me.

"Didn't they do an amazing job?" she asked, but didn't wait for a reply, "And the food, Marci, you are going to love the food. But go mingle." She squeezed my arm. "Maybe one of your girlfriend's boyfriends have a friend they can link you up with." She patted my arm and walked away.

I took a deep breath and went straight to the bar to grab a glass of wine to accompany me on my walk around the restaurant. Thanks to the drinks, the music, and laughing with my girls, my mama's stunt was just about forgotten.

Then I sat down at my designated place at the table, and noticed the empty seat beside me—unoccupied, even after everyone found their place. The appetizers were passed, the drinks were topped off, and my mom stood to toast me. When she sat down, Nic leaned over and asked, "Should I be toasting to your spirit boyfriend beside you?" I reached under the table and flicked her leg as I shook my head and rolled my eyes.

CHAPTER FOUR

JOSEPH

"Yo." Alonzo tapped my arm. "Isn't that the girl you were supposed to be taking out?" I stopped in the middle of the sidewalk and looked over my shoulder. "Naw, over there." He nodded his head across the street. "Walking out of the nail shop."

I narrowed my eyes, but I couldn't get a good glimpse of her face. She had already moved down the sidewalk. "I didn't see her face." I didn't know why I was even trying, she didn't seem interested, at all. "Not like it matters," I mumbled.

Alonzo laughed then tapped me on my chest with the back of his hand. "Sounds like somebody got his little feelings hurt." I was trying to remember why Alonzo and I hung out after work. "Let me know, I can be your wingman."

I shook my head and looked across the street again, but if it was Marcia, she was nowhere in sight.

"Right now, how about we just grab this paint." I opened the door to the hardware store. "I'm starting to get hungry."

We walked the aisles of the paint section, neither of us agreeing on a color. "This"—he held up a paint swatch—"royal blue is hitting."

I shrugged. "The whole office?" We were supposed to be fixing up our space, the one that was starting to look a little raggedy—paint peeling, dim lighting, rusty chairs. "I just can't see four whole walls being dark blue."

"Sounds like you two could use some help." That voice sounded familiar, and when I turned around and saw Marcia's face, I was a little surprised to see her in the hardware store. "What are you trying to paint?" She smiled at me then looked at Alonzo and gave him a similar smile.

Alonzo ate that shit up. His face grew into a wide grin, and he said, "We definitely could use some help." Then he asked, "What's your name?" And I questioned everything he'd ever told me, because the way he asked her for her name like he didn't know damn well who she was, was way too smooth.

My eyes widened as I watched her extend her hand to him. "Marcia, nice to meet you." She paused for him to repeat his name. "And I already know your friend here." She turned to me.

"Okay, Marcia, Jo and I were looking for some paint for our office." But the way she paused and looked at me, it was like she was no longer interested in helping us find paint. Her eyes, as beautiful as they were, had narrowed, and the smile on her face had faded.

Alonzo noticed it too, but instead of letting it slide, he asked, "You okay?"

She turned to him and nodded. "Yeah, of course." She pointed to the royal blue he was holding and offered, "But that's way too dark." Her eyebrow hitched. "You should look for something warm, more neutral." She picked up a light brown and handed it to him. "Like this." And as if there would be no question, she walked away.

Alonzo shrugged and said, "Grant Beige it is," to her retreating back. "What are you waiting for?" He looked over his shoulder. "Go get the girl." Then he laughed. "Or fuck around and lose her to the better man." He popped his collar. "She did give me that cute smile." Before he could go on, I left him alone on the aisle.

I went down the main aisle, looking down each of the rows. While my head turned, I thought about how I could approach her again. Then I saw her with a hammer in her hand. "Are you doing some work too?" I said as she looked over the selection of nails. She looked at me and smiled. "You offered to help with the paint, how about I offer to help with your project?"

She laughed then asked, "You sure about that?" I nodded my head. "I have to hang a few pictures in my condo." I shrugged.

I grabbed my stomach and offered a compromise. "I'm starving, though, would you mind grabbing dinner with me first?" She hesitated, and I added, "I know, our first interaction was suspect, but if you are open to it, I'd like to act like that didn't happen."

"I can definitely put it out of my mind, if you can." I nodded. Then she looked over her shoulder. "But aren't you painting your office?"

I narrowed my eyes. "Now?" Then laughed, "No, maybe this weekend." Then I looked beyond her and said, "Let me grab the paint, though, and I'll meet you back here in like fifteen minutes."

She nodded and continued looking at the nails. Alonzo was already at the register. "I got it, bruh, you can get me later," he shouted as I walked toward him. "I'll catch up with you tomorrow." He grabbed the bags and headed for the exit.

I walked back toward Marcia, and she was still standing in front of the nails. "Don't know which nails you need?" She shook her head. "Are the pictures heavy?" She winced. "How heavy?"

"Maybe twenty pounds." I asked her if she was sure about that. "Yes, they aren't pictures exactly." She dug her phone from her purse. "They are these wooden carvings." She showed me a picture on her phone, and they were elaborate, intricate detail, and thick.

"Got it, okay, then we'll need some anchors, and..." I started grabbing what we'd need from the shelf. "This should do it." When we made it to the register, I pulled out my wallet.

"Oh no," she said from behind me as she dug through her purse. "You don't have to do that." But I ignored her and paid anyway. When we were outside I offered to drive us across town to the restaurant. "I just assumed we'd hit one of these restaurants on Main Street." I shook my head.

"No, I like to mix it up a bit." She frowned. "You don't like variety?"

"I do, but if you drive I'll still need to come back to get my car then go back to my place." I looked down at my watch. "I don't know if I'm up for all that tonight."

"I have a better idea." I nodded my head. "How about I meet you at your house then we order delivery?" Her eyes widened. "What, do you not eat food in your house?" I joked.

She rolled her eyes then said, "We just met." I mouthed okay, then she added, "That's not a little too much?"

"If I told you I was having you for dessert, maybe, but sharing a meal in your home..." I shrugged. "Seems fine."

Her coffee-brown skin concealed her blush, but the way her eyes fluttered, I knew she was flattered. "I guess you're right," she conceded.

"What would you like to eat?" Marcia had a badass body, one I assumed she crafted through hard work in the gym and a strict diet. So when she answered she wanted a salmon salad, with dressing on the side, I wasn't surprised. "Got it, I'll order it now. See you at your place?" She nodded before disappearing down the street.

On my way to my car, I placed our order and thought about how the evening was unfolding. I wasn't surprised that I bumped into Marcia. I'd seen her around town before, but our worlds just never collided.

She mentioned the same as I stood on the ladder in her living room with the twenty-plus-pound woodcarving. "How is it we never met before?"

I couldn't really respond because I had a nail sticking out of my mouth. I shrugged, and mumbled, "Good question." She went on to ask if I grew up in Rolling Hills.

After knocking the nails into the wall, then balancing the carving on them, I replied, "I did, I graduated from Hill High." Her eyes narrowed. "A few years before you, if I remember correctly."

"Wait." She crossed her arms across her chest. "You know me?"

I climbed down off the ladder. "Who doesn't know The Mercy Girls?" Her mouth opened slightly, and I didn't know who was more shocked—her or me for her not knowing she was a local celebrity. Or at least her dad was. "Your dad..." Before I could finish, she nodded her head.

"Of course." Then she sighed. "Mr. Rolling Hills himself." We both laughed. "I was active in high school, thought I knew just about everyone." She narrowed her eyes. "I definitely think I'd remember an older, fine brother like yourself." She took me in like she was drinking a tall glass of iced tea—nice and slow, savoring each sip.

"By the time you were coming through, I was likely not around as much." Her eyebrows bunched together, and I explained, "I did work study." She nodded slowly. "And," I laughed, "not sure if I would have fallen into that description in high school."

"No?" I shook my head. "Hmm..." She looked at me then turned to the next carving to be hung. "We should get this one up and maybe have that dessert you ordered."

We had devoured the food as soon as it arrived. Well, I did, she ate small bites, and half her plate was stored away in the fridge. "Yeah, that dessert." Then I asked, "But are you going to eat more than one small bite?" She wagged her head. "It's still your birthday month, right?"

"It is." She smiled softly. "Maybe a few bites won't hurt."

"Good," I said as I made my way back up the ladder. "How was your birthday party anyway?" I looked down as her eyes grew wide, and she described how, "fabulous," her party was. But then she groaned, and I looked down and saw her face distorted into a grimace. "Whoa, what's that about?"

"Obviously, you know my mom." She paused then shook her head. "She is very determined to have things her way. And although she went all out for my birthday, she harped on the fact that I am still single."

"Tell me more about that," I insisted.

She shrugged. "Not much to tell honestly." But after I asked her to elaborate, she admitted, "I've been single for a few years now." She looked around her condo then back up to me and said, "Maybe since college actually."

I quickly did the math, and then said, "Oh."

Then she clarified, "Well, I haven't been in a committed relationship since I graduated and we went our separate ways." The second woodcarving was on the wall and stable. I climbed off the ladder, and when she said, "Since then, it's just been random dudes who haven't been able to keep my attention," we were in each other's personal space.

"Is that right?" I asked, lowering my voice from the shout I had on top of the ladder.

She nodded then quickly diverged, asking me, "But what about you?"

"Me and my ex broke up last year." Her eyes grew wide. "That's actually how I ended up back in Rolling Hills."

She sauntered to the dining room table, her ass floating behind her. "Tell me more about *that.*"

Because we were both in Rolling Hills, where we grew up, I knew she was familiar with the small town struggle I felt constantly. "I thought we would get married, and when I found out she didn't have the same plans, I needed a change." I didn't elaborate on my dad's condition, and my mom insisting I come home to help with his business.

"So, Rolling Hills?" she asked, and I could sense the sarcasm in her tone. Even with her back to me, I knew she had a smirk on her face.

I sat across from her at the table and nodded my head. "So, Rolling Hills." I cocked my head. "But can't be that bad, right?" Her eyebrow hitched. "Then why are you here?"

"That's a longer story than either of us have time for right now." She looked down at her watch. "I have an early start in the morning," she politely reminded me that it was a Thursday night, and I, too, needed to be up at the crack of dawn.

"Right." I rolled my neck and declared, "Week's not quite over yet." I opened the container, and the cheesecake—drizzled in strawberry sauce and chunks of berries—almost looked too good to eat.

Marcia grabbed two forks and handed one to me. "If we have to be in Rolling Hills, might as well make the best of it, right?" I nodded my head because I couldn't agree more.

"This wouldn't exactly be my idea of a first date." I looked into her brown eyes and continued as she wrapped her mouth around a bite of cheesecake. "I'd love to take you out on a proper date."

She covered her mouth, finishing her chew before she agreed, "Not a bad idea."

I dug my phone out of my pocket and joked, "Unless we are going to bump into each other at the hardware store again, I should probably get your phone number." After she rattled off her number, I stood from the table and walked my fork over to her sink. "I'm going to get out of here, but if you're up for it, I'll call you tomorrow."

"Tomorrow works for me." She smiled wide. She held the door open as I walked out, but before I made it too far down the hall, she said, "Thank you for your help tonight." I waved, and she closed the door.

CHAPTER FIVE

MARCIA

"So, the man Mama hooked you up with?" Liv repeated on the phone.

"The one you told to kick rocks when he showed up at your place a few weeks ago?" Nic joked.

"Ugh," I sighed. "Remind me again why I have these group calls with you two," I said as I placed the phone on my bathroom counter. "Get the two of you together and it's a whole comedy show."

"Okay, for real." Liv cleared her throat. "So, he's back in Rolling Hills." She was repeating everything I had just given them a run down on. "And he does what exactly?"

I thought about our conversation from the night before and realized I had no idea. "I don't know actually."

"What?" Nic shouted. "You don't have his entire resume in PDF format stored to your phone?" I sighed but didn't have to say anything because Liv warned Nic they needed to be serious. "Right, because after all, Mama could get her way and this could be our future brother-in-law." She scoffed, "Imagine that shit."

Then Liv chimed in, "Lisa Mercy always gets her way."

I added, "One way or another."

"Anyway, if you let the man in your house on the first night, he must have some mojo that the rest of these dudes were lacking." I laughed because it wasn't like I let him in my bedroom, and I made sure she knew that. "Oh, I know, Ms. Keeping the Goods Locked Up Till Marriage." She started rambling on about how, "It couldn't be her, celibate and horny. Nope."

Then I corrected her, "I'm not celibate." I looked in the mirror at my red lips. "Horny, yes. But I'm not about to be out here spreading love and still end up lonely by the end of the month."

Liv interrupted, "That's right, because every person you lay down with, you collect their energy, give them yours."

"Listen," Nic cackled, "you just don't know what that energy will do for you."

"Okay, so on that note…" I grabbed my phone, ready to click the end call button. "I'll call you two tomorrow."

"Tomorrow?" they shouted in unison as I said goodbye and hung up.

Before I left the bathroom, I ran my finger across my braided bun. For our real date, Joseph said he was surprising me, and when I asked what I should wear, he said something comfortable. I was skeptical. I decided on high-waisted joggers and a tank, hoping that I could fit in if we decided to be in a restaurant or outdoors somewhere. I slid on a pair of neon sneakers, and felt I was rocking the hell out of *casual*.

Joseph was punctual—a few minutes before seven o'clock and I heard a knock at the door. "You know, you are racking up points by being on time."

He grinned then asked, "What exactly do I win with these points?"

I cocked my head as I pulled the door shut behind me, then locked it. "Hmm, we'll just have to see how many you get." He laughed. "It'll be like the game room, there has to be levels to this." I didn't think he could laugh any harder, but he did, and when I looked up at him, the smile that remained after was sexy. His beard, and the way it framed his mouth, his beautiful white teeth, contrasting skin, and those eyes—I was feeling all of that.

"You good?" he asked as he walked beside me out of my building. I nodded my head, and he said, "You are looking at me all, tantalizing."

I snapped my head back. "Okay, five-dollar word."

"Nice try with that deflection tactic."

And he caught me. "No, I was just admiring how sexy you are." He shook his head. "Anyway, where are we headed?"

"Do you always do that?"

"What?" I scrunched my brows.

"Deny yourself pleasure." I was completely lost, so lost I had to stop walking.

He stopped beside me then said, "If I'm sexy, you must have thought otherwise when I could have been your date to your party. And just now, you skipped right on past any response I could have given you."

Right then, in that hallway, on the way to who knows where, I knew Joseph was different. I thought about what he said then asked, "What type of response is due to that statement anyway?"

His tongue licked out across his lips, and he stared at me until I could feel his gaze deep inside my belly. Then he reached his hand out and his knuckle brushed against my cheek. My eyes fluttered closed, then back open, and when they opened, he replied, "That." Then he led me to the car where we rode listening to jazz music.

"I don't know what I expected to hear on your radio, but..." He looked at me with his eyebrows raised as we sat at the red light. "I didn't expect jazz."

"Tell me more," he insisted. Being a lover of the arts, music was my thing. In high school, I was in the concert band and thought I'd become a famous violinist.

"I don't know." I stared at him, his demeanor softening the more I looked past his tall frame and chiseled features. "Maybe Kendrick Lamar." He laughed.

"That's so very specific." He pulled away from the red light, and as we drove further outside of the city, I asked where we were headed. "Just trust me," he murmured, and at first it sounded like the last words of a serial killer, but then I felt my body ease into the seat when he added, "I promise it's worth it."

We pulled into the state park, and I looked down at my sneakers. "Glad I decided not to wear any heels," I mumbled more to myself than to him.

"Don't worry, we aren't hiking through the woods." He paused then clarified, "Not tonight anyway." I raised my brows because I likely would not ever be hiking in the woods. Me and the outdoors were not close friends, more like distant acquaintances—brunch on a covered patio, yes; hiking in the woods, absolutely not. But I smiled as he hopped out of the car. I had my hand on the door handle when I saw him appear and shake his head. "Really? Did I not open your door when you climbed in?" I shrugged. "Last dude had to be trash." I laughed because, yeah, maybe he was a little trash. I attributed it to him being young, us being young, and not really knowing what to do in a real relationship. "I'd think a woman like you would have high standards."

I narrowed my eyes and crossed my arms across my chest. "What does that mean?" I asked as we walked side-by-side into the darkness.

He wagged his head then answered, "Manicured nails, hair on point, face made up, clothes from the city's exclusive boutique." He looked down at my sneakers and continued, "Even your sneakers, exclusive."

"Okay?" I egged him on.

"A woman like you who obviously takes care of herself doesn't demand the man in her life do the same?"

My nose scrunched up, and I quickly replied, "I'm not sure what you are implying, but all I'm feeling is judged." He stopped walking and looked at me, his skin blending in with the darkening sky, his eyes hardly leaving mine.

"Don't feel judged, it's an observation. But let me take care of you as much as you take care of you." He lowered his head. "Deal?" I nodded my head and he placed a kiss on my cheek. "Good." He reached for my hand. "Gotta make sure we don't trip over anything out here."

He guided us into an open area with a fire pit blaring and, surprisingly, other couples paired off sitting around it. "What is this?"

"There's a catering company." I looked to the side and saw the tent and tables and a few people shuffling beneath it. "A few nights a week they come out here and cater dinner, near the pit."

I brushed my hands across my arms and considered how many bugs were likely swarming around. But I kept it simple and said, "Interesting concept."

We found a set of chairs and sat across from each other. "I hope you don't mind that our first"—he put his hands in the air and wagged them—"date isn't at a fancy restaurant."

I rolled my eyes and shook my head. "C'mon, that's not an observation." I paused. "That's definitely a judgment, or an assumption at least." I looked around the fire pit at the other couples laughing and talking, sipping on drinks. "Maybe I'm not the great outdoorsy type, but I'm open to new experiences." I smiled. "And this is definitely a new experience."

"Good, because there is only so much we can do in Rolling Hills to keep it fresh." I nodded in agreement. A server approached us, running down the drink menu, then told us the two options for dinner. "I'll have a bourbon, neat. And the steak." Then he looked at me.

"I'll have a glass of the white wine." The server nodded, then I added, "And the seafood pasta." When she walked away, I looked at Joseph and asked, "What other fresh adventures have you been on lately?"

He started to tell me, "Since being back, I picked up hiking again." He looked off into the darkness where I knew there were never-ending trees, and likely accompanying wildlife. "And fishing." I bit the inside of my lip to keep myself from frowning. Neither of those sounded like fresh ideas.

"Anything that doesn't involve nature?"

He took his time to respond. "At least every other month I'm flying out to a different city I've never been to."

I grinned. "That's the type of adventure I like. What's the last city you visited?"

"Cartagena."

"Cartagena?" He nodded his head. "Like Colombia?" He nodded again. "Wow. It hasn't been on the top of my list of places to visit, but how was it?"

"It's a beautiful city, different from any other place I've been." The server dropped off our drinks, and he took a sip of his bourbon while I held onto my glass, swirling the wine around. "Beautiful people, vibrant culture, and the food is definitely on point." It was almost as if he was revisiting, because his smile grew with each word he spoke. "I'd go back for the Pan de Bono alone."

I couldn't be mad at his love of food, because I was a fan myself. "I've never heard of it, but now I feel like I should book a trip." We both laughed. Then he asked about the last place I visited, and I felt it paled in comparison. "Arizona."

"How was it?" He explained how he hadn't been but heard the spas were worth being in the hot ass sun.

"Definitely worth it. I actually went for a wellness retreat." I smiled, remembering Liv convincing us we needed to rejuvenate after her first year working full time. "I'd go again if you are down for a trip."

"Look at you, trying to book a trip." He licked his tongue across his lips. "Does that mean I'm definitely getting another date?"

Sexy as fuck—check. Adventurous and world traveled—check. Treats me right—check. I couldn't stop myself when I responded, "Hell yeah." And he just laughed.

CHAPTER SIX

JOSEPH

I took the last sip of my bourbon and placed my cup on the ground. I leaned forward and placed my hand on her knee. She put hers on top of mine and said, "Thank you. This was nice." Softly, her lips closed in a pucker and had me wanting to take them into my mouth.

"You're welcome." We stared at each other for a minute before I asked, "Are you ready to leave?" She nodded her head then looked around. "Thinking about coming back for a hike, aren't you?"

I was joking but was surprised when she answered, "Maybe."

"Oh shit." My eyes widened and I stood from my seat. I reached my hand out to help her rise too. "Better get you out of here before you become a full-on outdoorsman."

She laughed and we made it back to the car, hand-in-hand. I opened her car door and thought about my next move. I didn't want to be the creep that pushed my way into her place on the first night, although I had already been in her place, but I didn't want her to think I was all about the sex. As I walked around to my side of the car, I thought of how I could get her up to her front door, but not seem like I was trying to make my way in.

I didn't have to think too hard because when I pulled into her parking garage, she asked, "Coming up?"

To which I replied, "Yeah," then looked at her, "gotta make sure you make it to your place safely."

Her eyes widened. "Okay." Then she softly giggled. I didn't ask her what that was all about. Instead, I opened her door and let her lead the way to the elevator.

We were the only ones in the elevator—standing closely—and I felt her fingers brush up against my hand. But she didn't intertwine our fingers. So, I did. Then I looked down at her as her floor approached and leaned into her space a little closer. I grabbed the back of her head and when her lips opened slightly, I let my tongue dip into her mouth.

I could have stayed just like that all night, but the elevator doors opened and she ended the kiss. "Hmm," she hummed as she stepped off of the elevator. I saw her rubbing her hand around her neck as we approached her front door.

"You okay?" I asked.

She stuttered, "Yeah, I ugh," as she fumbled for her keys. Then she turned and looked at me. "I um..."

Before she could finish, I stretched my arms wide and wrapped them around her. I felt her hands rest on my waist. Then I whispered in her ear, "Have a good night," before I turned and walked back to the elevator.

When I made it back to my place, before I could even get comfortable, I sent a text message.

Joseph: Thank you

My mom quickly replied, and I told her I'd call her in the morning. She was likely up late watching re-runs of some old soap opera. The next text I sent was to Marcia. I didn't have plans for the second date, but I wanted her to know I wanted one. I wanted more time with her.

Marcia: Tomorrow?

We coordinated a time, all through text, but then I called her. "Everything okay?" she said, but sounded like she was holding her breath.

"Yeah, I just wanted to hear your voice again." I laughed to myself because if any of my friends had told me they did that, I'd clown the hell out of them. But there I was, being corny as fuck for this woman.

"Oh, okay." I heard water running in the background. "I was just about to climb into the shower." Then it stopped. "But I have a few minutes for you."

"Shower, huh," I repeated, "I'm going to act like you didn't say that so you in the shower isn't the last thought on my mind, or I definitely won't be going to bed tonight."

She laughed, harder than I ever heard her laugh before. And she continued until she took a breath and said, "Had you not rushed off, this conversation could have been in person."

"Rushed off?" I tapped my leg. "You were looking a little flustered, so I didn't want you to feel any pressure to invite me in."

"It's not like you haven't been in my place before, but I do have this random rule." My head fell back and I thought how everything up until that point was probably too good to be true. I braced myself for her to say something that made her out of reach, or undesirable. But she left me hanging when she said, "But if I shared that random rule with you, it'd be like breaking the rule."

"Okay," I said slowly. "Just as long as you know the rule and don't change it up mid-game."

"Huh," she huffed, "if you can make it mid-game, believe me, there will be no switching it up."

"I don't know if I ever wanted to play a game more," I joked. "I'll let you get back to your shower."

"Have a good night, Joseph." I committed the way she said my name to memory—the only thing I could imagine was her screaming it out with just as much passion.

"Good night, Marcia." I made myself go to bed after that. But the next morning, I woke up with Marcia on my mind.

I called my mom. "Good morning, ol' lady," I said with a smile, waiting for her to remind me she was the definition of youth.

"Boy, you know I'm nowhere near old. Now what were you talking about last night, 'thank you' for what?"

She didn't waste any time. "I took Marcia out on a date."

Then she showed her age, and her horrible memory. "That's good, baby, but why are you thanking me?" I could hear the birds chirping because she was likely in her garden. I reminded her that Marcia was the girl she set me up with. "Oh, of course, I knew you would figure it out."

"Oh, you knew that, huh?" Then she threw a low jab and told me not to mess it up. "Dang, Mom, I didn't mess up the last relationship."

"That's your story, and you are *really* sticking to it." I didn't tell my mom that my ex cheated on me. I didn't feel it was necessary, but had I known she would have been riding so hard for her, I would have given her all the details. "You coming over today?" Then I heard her curse under her breath. "Can't let these bugs destroy my garden," she proclaimed loudly.

"I'll stop by before I head out." She tried to guilt me by reminding me that the reason I moved home was to be closer to her. "That's right, but aren't you the same person who said I needed to find a woman?"

"Oh, absolutely, and make her your wife too. But before you get too lost in all that, don't forget you have your mama here." Then she started talking crazy and I had to hurry off the phone. "Really, bring her to meet me."

"Not today." Before she could start complaining, I said, "I'm headed to the gym. I'll see you later, Mama."

Since being back home, I'd been in the gym with the guys almost every Saturday morning. We would join a pick-up game with some of the younger dudes in the community. When I walked into the gym, I saw Chris and Alonzo chatting it up in the bleachers as a few guys ran up and down the court. "What happened?" I said, pointing to the court.

"Oh, we got next," Alonzo said after yawning. "We were waiting on you."

I nodded and sat beside Chris, who wasted no time getting in my business. "Zo told me you kicking it with one of the Mercy sisters." He was staring me down, as if my answer could save his life.

But I looked to Alonzo, who tried to avoid eye contact. "Yeah," I responded simply. I didn't know Chris when I was in high school, but the way he kicks it with us now, you'd think he had been hanging with us since we were kids.

Alonzo looked at Chris and laughed. "I didn't tell him which one." I looked between the both of them, confused. "Chris has been trying to lock down Nicolette for years." That didn't clarify anything. "She's Marcia's younger sister."

I nodded my head, then Chris smiled. "Oh, so you're dating Marcia?" His eyes widened. "She's an interesting one."

"What?" I narrowed my eyes. "What do you mean she's an interesting one?" I repeated.

He elaborated, "I don't know, man, she's bourgeois as all get out." I thought back to the night before and her hesitance to go into the woods, but I wasn't getting bourgeois vibes, more scared, maybe. "And stuck in her ways. That's why she's been single all these years." And that part stuck with me, because she did mention it had been a while since her last relationship. As much as I wanted to hear more of his opinion of Marcia, we had next.

I hopped off the bleachers and onto the court. Running up and down between plays, I thought about the plans I had for our next date—bowling. Then I thought about what Chris was saying about Marcia being bourgeois and thought maybe I should change my plans. "Naw," I whispered to myself as I shot a three-pointer from mid-court.

If she was too good to bowl, then maybe we didn't belong together. We ended up getting wiped out in the game, and Alonzo tried to blame me. "Man, where the hell were you today?" I looked at him sideways, considering he missed fifty percent of the shots he put up. "I mean, you usually come in beasting."

"I don't know, man," I admitted, "Maybe the youngins are finally getting better." I watched the teens across the court celebrating their first win against us. "Let them have it this once, but next week, I'm on my shit," I warned.

"Ay man," Chris said as we were leaving the court, "how about you, me, Nicolette, and Marcia go out on a double date?"

Alonzo laughed hard. "Doesn't that mean that Nicolette has to be willing to go out with you?"

Chris shook his head but kept talking up his plans for a double date. "We take them to Everson's, I know they'd like that." Everson's was one of the most expensive restaurants in Rolling Hills. I had been there a few times with my parents—to mark special occasions like graduation, my mom's retirement—my mom and I even went when I moved back home. But I hadn't really considered it for a date with Marcia, it seemed cliché.

But Chris wouldn't shut up, so I said, "Maybe one day, man."

CHAPTER SEVEN

MARCIA

My sisters were relaxing on my couch when my phone vibrated. "Oh, who could that be?" Liv asked with a smile.

I didn't respond and just grabbed my phone and opened my messages.

Joseph: Bowling tonight?

When Joseph asked for another date, I was all game. But I had to admit his choices were—different. I had just finished telling my sisters about our time in the woods, and although it turned out to be super romantic, it wasn't anything I'd expect.

So when I blurted out, "Bowling?" They both looked at each other and laughed. "What do I wear to the bowling alley?"

"Dude is taking you all the way out your comfort zone. Two days without a pair of heels?" Nic looked at me with her head cocked. "How will you survive?"

I shook my head and shot her a look. "I don't always have to wear heels," I defended myself. "I have a diverse wardrobe."

"Spoken like a true queen." They both laughed. "But for real, have you ever even been bowling?" Nic asked.

I sighed, and said, "Of course." The last time I had been bowling was likely with the two of them, when we were all kids, but, of course, I had been bowling.

"You don't sound so sure about that." Liv grabbed her glass and took a sip. "I can't wait to hear about this date."

"But what I really want to hear about is if you are going to drop the panties tonight."

Liv looked to Nic and shook her head. "You know this woman and her rules." I was proud of my little sister for remembering. But when she joked, "Those panties have a pad lock and the key is likely lost by now it's been so long."

My mouth dropped open. "Here I was thinking you were the sweet one." I stood from the couch and added, "I don't even know why I always have you around. I swear I have a group of girlfriends who aren't so critical."

"But who needs them when you have us?" Nic was extra elaborate with her hands waving in the air. I rolled my eyes and made my way to the kitchen where I texted Joseph back.

Marcia: Sure

He shot back a few texts asking about times, and we finally agreed on seven o'clock. I had to find a way to get my sisters off my couch so they wouldn't be there when he arrived. The last thing I needed was for them to be around grilling him. "Didn't you say you had to go by Mom's house?" I asked, standing in front of my open fridge.

"Yes," Liv groaned. "She has some project she needs my help on." Liv was the creative one out of all of us. "I told her we have an entire staff of graphic artists, but yet here I am, doing their job too."

"Couldn't be me," Nic said.

And Liv shot back, "You're right, because you couldn't draw to save your life." She stood from the couch. "Let me get over there so I can still hit the club tonight."

"Hey..." Nic stood behind her, and I was happy she was going to leave too. "You didn't tell me you were going out tonight."

I turned from the fridge to watch their interaction. Liv bit her lip, and I knew she was about to come up with some lie. But I was surprised when she answered honestly, "I mean, when is the last time you were at the club? Besides, you don't really like my homegirls like that." Nic shrugged then plopped back down on my couch as Liv continued to the front door. "I'll catch you two later, and Marcia..." She stuck her head around the corner. "Call me if he gets the goods." She laughed and walked out the door.

"Here I am," Nic sighed, "single, and no plans for the night. Who would have thought?" She pouted.

I reminded her, "You could always give Chris a call." Then I laughed, but Nic didn't find that funny at all. Chris was her yo-yo, they went back and forth more than any couple I knew. "Oh, you off again this week?"

"Off for forever." She frowned then repeated, "Forever." She grabbed my remote then said, "Maybe there's a Lifetime movie on."

"Ma'am," I interrupted her scrolling, "don't you have cable at your place?"

Her eyes bulged. "Oh, now you got a man and you are kicking me to the curb?" She gasped. "I can't believe it." She snatched up her purse and shook her head. "And you ain't even gettin' the dick yet," she huffed as she walked past me.

I laughed then yelled, "I'll call you later," to her back as she walked out of my front door.

I went into my closet and scrutinized each piece of clothing—nothing was giving me bowling vibes. My shoulders slumped and

I sighed. I shuffled through my racks again, and finally found a well-fitting pair of jeans and a crop top that would be perfect. I figured I would need a pair of socks to put my feet into the borrowed shoes, but my heels were calling out to me. "Next time," I whispered as I grabbed a pair of retro sneakers, "I promise."

I hurried to the bathroom and turned on the spray of water until the bathroom was steamy. I had a bun the night before, but I decided to go with a low ponytail for the bowling alley. Before I got into the shower, I glanced at my phone, about thirty minutes until Joseph would be knocking at the door. I hopped in and lathered up.

Just as I was buttoning my pants, I heard a knock at the door. I looked in the mirror and whispered, "Shit." I hadn't even put any makeup on yet. But I didn't want to keep him waiting too long, so I hurried to the door, and when I opened it, I didn't expect to see him looking fine as fuck in a retro bowling shirt, but that was him, and he was wearing the hell out of the shirt. "Hey." I motioned for him to come inside. "I was just finishing up." I didn't mention the fact that he was a little early.

I also didn't notice anything in his hands until he said, "Hey, here you go." He held out a bouquet of flowers. "Is this Marcia with a fresh face?" he asked, staring down at me. "Wow."

Hardly anyone ever saw me with a fresh face, I made sure of that. But the way he was looking down at me like he could gobble me up had me wanting to reconsider—at least for him anyway. "You okay?" I asked as I walked into the kitchen to grab a vase for the roses. "And thank you, these are beautiful." I placed them onto the kitchen counter.

"Yeah, not that I expected you to look different without makeup, but..." He licked his lips. "Just, wow." He shrugged his shoulders. "I'll sit over here while you finish, if you don't mind." I nodded my head and floated back to my bathroom. I grabbed the eyeliner, mascara, and a little gloss—and that was it. When I returned, he said, "Retro Nikes," with a slow head nod. "You are full of surprises."

I didn't expect him to notice my sneakers. "Guess we are both full of surprises." I plucked at his shirt. "Ready to roll?"

"Now," he warned as we walked to the elevator, "I'm a little competitive, so I hope you don't expect I'll let you win."

Then that's when I had to burst his competitive bubble and inform him, "Don't worry, you'd have to try too hard to let me win." I squinted. "It's been a really long time since I bowled last."

His mouth dropped open. "You mean Rolling Lanes wasn't your hangout spot as a teen?" I shook my head. "What were you doing in high school?"

"I was a cheerleader." He shrugged. "And I hung out at the mall." He nodded his head. "And the library."

"The library?" he repeated. "You *hung out* at the library?" I nodded my head. "Was that some name for a teen club or something?" He narrowed his eyes.

"No," I laughed. "I was determined to get into college on a full ride." He nodded his head slowly, and I'm sure he was trying to make sense of it. "It wasn't necessary, but it was a personal goal."

"Ambitious," was all he said in response. "It's time for you"—he tapped my hand—"to make up for lost times. These next few dates," he paused and looked at me, but I was waiting for him to finish, "will be all things you likely missed out on in this little town as a teenager."

I laughed, because the idea sounded crazy, but the look on his face was serious. "Next dates, huh?" His eyebrow rose. "I admire your confidence." We both laughed.

After my third attempt at knocking down pins—and failing—Joseph pulled me aside and said, "I'm not sure I ever met anyone who wasn't able to knock down a *single* pin." I groaned. "Okay, we have to get in the game." He looked beside us to the lanes packed with families, and other couples likely on a date. "This is what we are going to do." He tugged me by the hand and brought me back to the balls. "Let's test out these balls." I cocked my head. "Yeah, that sounded terrible." He handed me a ball. "How is that?" I shrugged because I didn't know what I was feeling for.

"I need a heavy ball to hit the pins hard, right?" His eyes narrowed and he shook his head. Then he explained that I needed a ball that I could throw easily. "Oh, then let's try something else." I rubbed my fingers after I removed them from the ball.

"Now," he said when I finally had a ball that was comfortable with my fingers, and wasn't too heavy for me to roll down the lane. "Straighten your arm." I did as he directed. "Lean forward a little more," then he warned, "not that far." I felt like I was learning how to drive, and my dad was in the passenger seat—the pressure was serious.

I took a deep breath and rolled the ball. As soon as it started making its way down the lane, I clenched my eyes closed. I heard pins falling but just knew it was the person beside me, until I heard Joseph yell and I felt his arms wrapped around me. "Look," he whispered in my ear, "you got a strike." I opened my eyes in time to see each of the pins be swiped to the back.

I turned around in his arms and kissed his cheek. "That was amazing." My heart was fluttering, and when he looked down at me I couldn't help but pull his head forward, my mouth on his, my lips parted and we kissed. In the middle of the bowling alley. I didn't care who was watching, or if I didn't know every detail about him, or what would happen next. I just kissed him and felt my body excite as his hands roamed my back.

"And that was too," he responded as he pulled away and looked deep into my eyes. "Now I have to keep the momentum before you try to come back and win." He winked.

CHAPTER EIGHT

JOSEPH

When I told Marcia I'd plan dates surrounding things she missed out on as a teenager, I was partially joking. Of course, I wanted to wine and dine her, but by the end of our bowling date, there was something different about her. Something relaxed, and at ease.

It had been a few days since we went bowling, and I didn't want to wait till the weekend to see her again. I was heading home from work when I shot her a text.

Joseph: Busy tonight?

A reply text never came, but by the time I made it to my place my phone was ringing. "Hey." Her voice sounded winded. "I just finished my workout."

"There's some place I want to take you," I paused, "if you are up for it."

"On a Wednesday night?" she blurted.

"On a Wednesday night, you and me." Then I added, "And a couple of race cars."

"Race cars?" Her voice hitched, and I already knew she likely hadn't been to Need for Speed, our infamous racecar track. "Ugh..." she hesitated.

"You don't even have to change out of your workout gear. I'll pick you up in about thirty minutes." And as much as I wanted to see her, I was starting to think she'd turn me down.

"Okay," she finally answered. Then when she threatened to beat my ass on the track, I could only laugh. "Don't worry, I know how to drive, and all I have to do is push the gas." She was overly confident.

"That's all you have to do," I said with a tight grin. "See you in thirty."

Biker shorts and a tank. Motherfucking biker shorts, and a tank. I couldn't think of anything else but her ass in those damn biker shorts. She looked over her shoulder and asked, "Everything okay?" as we made our way down to the track.

I cleared my throat and tried to look off into the distance—far away from her ass. "Yeah, everything is good."

"You sure?" She laughed.

Then I had to be honest. "If I had known your workout wardrobe consisted of tight biker shorts, maybe I would not have suggested you rock that."

Her eyes narrowed, and she asked with a sly grin, "Why is that?"

My head leaned to the side. "Because I'm trying to be a gentleman." Then I quickly looked away as she climbed into the car. But I looked back to see the young kid who was helping her in with his eyes wide open. "Yo," I said to distract him while she buckled up. "This me?" I pointed to the car parked in front of me, obviously my ride. He narrowed his eyes and nodded his head. "Bet."

There weren't many other people lined up to race, just a few teens likely not even licensed to drive. "Keep your hands in the car at all times," the kid started to announce, but as he continued, Marcia looked at me and winked.

She flew out ahead of me like she was at the Indy 500. She hit that turn and slowed all the way down, and as I passed her, I nodded. We continued edging each other out, until the last leg when she hit the straightaway and blew past me.

"Well, damn," I mumbled to myself.

"Told you all I had to do was keep my foot on the gas." She bit her lip.

I admitted defeat then looked toward the building and offered, "But how are you at arcade games?" She laughed and shook her head. "Up for trying?" Each game we played, or she tried to play, was a mixture of me explaining the rules to her, and her thinking she knew exactly how to win the most tickets.

"We should take these and give them to the youngest kid in here," she said, holding our bucket of tickets in the air.

"That sounds better than me taking them in there and grabbing you the biggest teddy bear possible." She scrunched her nose up.

"I don't know the last time I laughed so hard." She was talking to me but her head was turned toward the car window. "In fact, I forgot all about my challenges from work."

"I'm glad you had fun." As I parked in her garage, I insisted, "I'll walk you up." She didn't hesitate as I opened her door and walked beside her into the building. But when we got to her door, we stood awkwardly, both of us not saying anything. "Uhm, if you're free this weekend..." I didn't have anything specific in mind, but I knew I wanted to see her.

She nodded her head then stood up on her tippy toes, and I felt her lips on mine. I wrapped my hands around her waist and pulled her in closer to me. Our kisses were deep, needy, and my hand felt the mounds of her ass. Her chest was swollen and I could feel her nipples through her thin tank top. As much as I wanted to respect her boundaries, I also wanted to take her to her bedroom, spread her legs, and dive deep inside.

When she pulled away and unlocked the door, I stood behind her waiting for her to tell me goodnight, but I was pleasantly surprised when she asked, "Do you want to come in?"

Did I? In that moment, there was nothing I wanted more. I followed her inside and she walked into her kitchen. "Want something to drink?" Her voice was casual, unbothered. "I have a bottle of Uncle Nearest." She had a glass in her hand. "Or a few bottles of wine."

"I'll take the Uncle Nearest." I noticed my voice dropped an octave, and I cleared my throat to try and recover. "I can't imagine you drinking whiskey," I said as she handed me a glass and poured one herself.

She laughed. "You know..." Her eyes narrowed. "It wasn't really my drink until I visited this resort that hosted a whiskey tasting, and my sisters insisted we try it out." Then she raised her glass and said, "And I'm all about supporting black-owned businesses, so cheers to that." She clanked her glass against mine and we both took a sip.

I was leaning against her kitchen counter, and she stepped between my legs. "Now," she said softly, "I think I'd like to get back to that kiss."

She could have said less. My lips were back on hers, our tongues tangled, and my hands roaming. With her between my legs I knew she felt what I felt, and when she softly moaned, I could hardly hold back. I pulled back from the kiss and asked, "Do you want anything more than this kiss?" I looked down at her as she bit her lip, briefly hesitating before nodding her head. "You sure?" I asked.

She nodded her head again then maneuvered herself out of my reach. "C'mon," she offered over her shoulder as she walked to her bedroom. Her ass in those biker shorts led the way, and I eagerly followed.

She kicked out of her shoes and sat at the edge of her bed. "I think..." She looked away from me. "I should probably take a shower first." Then I remembered she had exercised before our racecar outing.

"Mind if I join you?" Although I was freshly showered, another round wouldn't hurt, especially if it was with her. She surprised me again when she shook her head.

She reached into the shower and started the stream of water, but then we both stood there looking at each other before she sighed. "Okay..." She gritted her teeth. "It's been a while since I've been with anyone." I knew her last boyfriend was years prior, but I didn't expect that it was also the last time she was intimate with anyone. I guess she could read my face, because she clarified, "I mean, not since my ex, long, but still." I nodded my head.

"Pretty sure it's like riding a bike." And when the words left my mouth, I couldn't take them back. She just laughed in response though. I stepped closer to her and grabbed at the hem of her shirt. "We can go as slow..." I grabbed her behind the head then kissed her lips before pulling apart and saying, "Or as fast as you want." With that, I lifted her shirt above her head and tossed it to the floor. Then I pulled off mine, and her eyes grew wide when she saw my bare chest. "We should probably get in before it gets cold, right?"

Her eyes briefly left my chest and she stuttered, "Right," before sliding off her shorts. Her bra and panties went behind them quickly. Both of us stood there, fully naked, for a beat, before we climbed into the shower. She avoided the spray of water and I stood in front of it to help her. I let my face be covered in the stream before I swiped it away and got busy on her body—she turned her back toward me and I massaged her shoulders, then rubbed soap down her back. When I reached her ass I could have stayed there forever.

Each time my hands connected with her body I could hear a soft whimper from Marcia. When I felt her back was clean, I scooted closer to her and let my hands drift down the front of her body. She rested her head on my chest, and I started a trail past her collarbone, to her chest, then finally to the valley between her legs. I stayed there until her moans sounded strained, and I continued down her legs before the water turned cool. "Let's step out," I whispered into her ear.

She grabbed a towel and passed one to me before she walked out to her bedroom. I followed behind her and watched as she climbed onto the bed. "You sure about this?" I asked as I stood in front of her bed, the towel wrapped around my waist.

She smiled, and then said, "I'm ready."

I grabbed the condom out of my wallet before I left the bath-room. "And so am I," I whispered as I rolled on the condom. I hovered over her, looking into her brown eyes. They wavered as I entered inside of her. Then she bit her lip before reaching up and pulling me down closer to her face.

She licked her tongue across her lips before she leaned in even closer and took my lips, biting on my lower lip as I pulled out, and entered back in. By the time our tongues met, I was in a groove. I found my rhythm and she was rocking with me, thrusting her hips when I backed away and bucking her back when I drew closer.

Between kisses and thrusts, I could hear her humming, and the sound was a beautiful melody. Then it stopped. Suddenly. And she moaned before shouting, "Dear God." I felt her legs shake, and her body went limp, her eyes closed tight.

I rocked a few more times before I collapsed beside her. "I have to go to work tomorrow." She rolled into my side and her head rested on my chest. "But I think I will have to call in." I laughed.

"I should probably go so you can get some rest," I told her without moving.

She interrupted the stillness by asking, "What now?"

Had she asked me that a few years prior, I'd likely bullshit my way around an answer. Instead, I responded, "We plan our next date."

CHAPTER NINE

Marcia

I sat at the conference room table, doodling on my notepad as I waited for my mother to make her appearance—who knew that fashionably late applied to business?

Anaya, one of my mom's assistants, sighed. "You okay?" I said when I looked up from my notebook.

Her eyes widened and she looked down before she finally replied, "Sorry." Then she looked at me and said, "I didn't mean for that to be heard by anyone else."

Nic joked, "It's alright, girl." She looked around the table at the other staff members and said, "I know we are all feeling it." She shrugged and focused her attention on me. "But you," she whispered, "don't seem to be bothered at all." I narrowed my eyes. "You can't still be riding that dick high?" Her mouth turned into a grimace. "You really need to get some more often."

I shook my head. "Really, Nic?" I looked around us at those likely hearing every word she was saying.

Then Liv chimed in from my other side. "I mean..." Her nose scrunched up. "Releasing that bottled up sexual energy is necessary." She laughed to herself. "It's like an oil change." She leaned in closer. "Imagine if your fancy car went *years* without an oil change." I looked between Liv and Nic and shook my head before ignoring them both.

Of course, my night with Joseph was amazing, and everything I needed. But that was never the problem. The problem was always what would happen next. The previous guys in my life had been trash. And they didn't start out as trash, but as soon as we had sex they transitioned into trash pretty quickly.

"You do know we are full adults now, right?" I looked to my side and saw Nic with her arms across her chest.

"What are you talking about?" I asked. But before she could respond, my mother sauntered into the room. I happened to look down the table at Anaya, who had a look of relief on her face, finally.

"Thank you all for waiting," my mother announced as if we had any other options. Her staff meetings were mandatory, and although my sisters or me could have easily walked out of the room, it'd set a bad example for all the other staff members patiently waiting. "Now, if you all haven't noticed..." She nodded toward Anaya, who started the presentation as my mom stood in front of the room and narrated. "Our sales are plateauing." I adjusted in my seat to examine the chart. "We're likely tapped out of our market audience." I looked to Nic because marketing was her department.

"I believe this launch of the men's line," my mom concluded, "will be exactly what we need to revitalize our sales." I wasn't a part of the day-to-day functions of the product team, but I had heard rumblings about the men's line they were designing.

Anaya passed around folders, packed with handouts and documentation. "Each of us should be well versed in our new offerings, and inside you'll find what you need specifically to focus on for the next couple of weeks." She asked if anyone had questions as she looked around the room slowly. She made eye contact with me before she cocked her head, then she continued her gaze around the room.

As we stood to leave, she said, "Marcia, dear." I turned to her and my eyebrows arched. "Have a second?" If I thought she was asking as the CEO of the company, I'd remind her that I should be busy telling my department about the impeding changes, but because I suspected she was asking as my mother, I nodded my head.

She examined my face, looking at each side then landing on my eyes before a grin spread over her face. "You changed your facial regimen lately?" I narrowed my eyes and shook my head. She put her finger to her chin then said, "Your face looks refreshed." She blinked a few times then finally asked, "Did you finally give that young man a chance?"

I hadn't shared anything about Joseph with her because I didn't want her getting excited about setting me up. I tempered her expectations by replying, "I did, actually." Then I added, "But Mom, I'm still upset about you feeling the need to intervene in my love life."

She laughed and lifted a hand in the air. "What love life, dear?" My eyes widened. "Not like that, it's just that since your ex you haven't given anyone a chance." I was channeling Anaya when I sighed, loudly. "Again, I apologize for making you feel some type of way." She lifted her hand to my cheek. "But if these are the results I get for intervening, then so be it." She kissed my cheek and then switched back into boss mode. "Now, get back to work."

I'd been anticipating the weekend since my night with Joseph. And as I shut down my computer for the day, I smiled thinking about seeing him again. "You're out of here already?" Anaya said as I passed her desk. I smiled and waved. "Wow."

I was usually in my office, or around the building, until six o'clock on a Friday evening. Walking out at four o'clock felt amazing. I had plans, other than sitting at home on the couch, or crashing at one of my sister's places. I tapped the elevator call button and when the doors opened, I stepped in with my head held high and happily rode down to the first level.

By the time I reached my car I had already entered weekend mode, removing my blazer before I sat behind the wheel. Rolling Hills didn't have many high-class restaurants, but that evening, I'd be sitting in one of the best. Finally, I had the chance to show Joseph the side of me that I enjoyed the most. Hair done, makeup flawless, dress tight, and heels high.

I spent the next couple of hours making sure my look was pulled together. But I couldn't decide if I was rocking my latest find from the boutique—a black dress with a low-cut neckline, or the red dress with a peek-a-boo back. I modeled each in the mirror before deciding to bet on red.

My earrings were in hand when I heard the knock at my door. "Shoot." I grabbed my clutch and slid into my heels. "Give me just a minute," I shouted at the door as I placed a diamond in each ear and took one last glance in the mirror. I was ready to remind Joseph of what he had a taste of earlier in the week.

But it was me whose mouth dropped when I opened the door. "Well, hello gorgeous," he said with a lick to his lips. Then the "Partition" lyrics were on repeat in my head, and I just stared and realized the past few hours could be in vain because we may not make it to the restaurant. "You good?" he asked.

I let my gaze drop to his shoes—the two-tone, brown, laced hard-bottoms. Then I followed the inseam of his perfectly fitting slacks to his imprint, and I squirmed before my eyes landed on his chest where the couple of buttons left undone almost had me undone. "Yeah," I finally responded, "I'm good."

His arms outstretched and he said, "Can I get a hug?" And his deep voice was even deeper. I looked up into his dark eyes and hesitated before I walked into his embrace. "Damn, girl, I think we have to skip out on the rest of the memory lane dates, and only do these grown and sexy ones from here on out." He pulled away slightly and his gaze traveled my body. "I didn't think it was possible for you to be any sexier." He shook his head and pulled me closer to him. "But gahtdamn." Before we departed from each other's arms, he nuzzled into my neck and left a kiss to make me run the lyrics back in my head once again.

"Let's go before we don't make it out of here," I warned.

He agreed, but as I turned to lock the door, I felt his body closer to mine. "Although..." I felt his arms on each side of the door surrounding me. "I don't know if that's exactly a bad thing." Then he kissed the back of my neck, and I felt every nerve ending in my body go on high alert.

I teased, "Not after I pulled all this on," with a swipe over my thighs. But then I felt a finger on my back, between the peek-a-boo cutout.

"All of this is right." And I felt his lips on my back before I heard steps down the hallway. But that didn't scare him, he stayed right where he was, unbearably close. "But you deserve to be seated at Rolling Hills's finest establishment." He snickered. "Hell, you deserve to be seated at a Michelin-star restaurant."

And I couldn't agree more. "Maybe one day." I smiled as I turned back to face him, and his lips landed on mine, but only briefly.

He stepped back and tugged on his blazer before reaching his hand out for mine. "Rolling Hills isn't ready for all this you giving tonight." We walked side-by-side to his car.

The restaurant was packed with the older, sophisticated crowd—the couples that were likely married for as long as either Joseph or I were alive; then there were a few younger couples like us. I smiled as we waited for the hostess to greet us, and I thought about the potential of Joseph and I being a couple, and the thought seemed *practical*.

He pulled out my chair, and I saw the older lady at the table beside us gently nod and smile as she watched us interact. Then when he sat across from me, the hostess informed us that our server would be there momentarily.

Our server, a beautiful black woman, announced, "Tonight, we are featuring a bottle of white wine from the Shooting Stars winery."

Joseph looked at me and shrugged before confirming, "We'll take a glass." When she walked away, he asked, "I almost forgot that winery was opened a few years ago, right?" I nodded my head. My family was good friends with the owners.

But I simply said, "I've been there a few times, and their wine is pretty good."

He didn't respond, just gently nodded. With his menu raised in front of him, he asked, "What do you think would pair well with their white wine?" I scanned the menu and suggested the risotto and scallops. "That actually sounds like a winner." His eyebrow raised as he sat his menu down.

"That was"—I cocked my head—"easy."

He looked beside us then back to me. "I'm sure we can't really go wrong with anything on the menu, and if you think it fits, then there's no need to keep looking." For some reason, I was thinking beyond the wine and risotto, and more into him and me.

"I think it fits," I responded softly, but my response was more about him and me than the wine pairing. We shared a glance before I looked down, closing my menu, and said, "I think I'll have the same, actually." His nose crinkled. "What?"

"There is no excitement if we both have the same entree." He grabbed his menu again, and as the server was delivering our glasses of wine, he asked, "What pairs well with this wine?"

She smiled and quickly told him, "The risotto." He shook his head and let her know that's what I was having. She looked between the two of us with a wider grin then said, "She's in luck then. For you, sir, how about the cranberry chicken and roasted potatoes?" He didn't seem as pleased with that choice but went with it anyway. "Would you all like to start off with the asparagus spears?" His eyebrows hitched up. "Or the crab dip?" He nodded to that. "If you need anything before then, please do not hesitate to ask."

"I know this is a fancy restaurant..." He adjusted his blazer. "But did she just ask me if I wanted asparagus spears?" My smile grew wide, but I tried not to laugh. "Do I look like a man who would enjoy asparagus spears?" I wagged my head. "No, the answer is no." He grabbed his chin and rubbed his hand across his beard. "I was most definitely the kid my mom had to bribe to eat my vegetables."

"Bless her heart," I said in my impression of a southern accent. "Do you have any siblings?"

"As a matter of fact"—he nodded his head—"I do. A younger sister who is," he sighed, "currently living in Tokyo."

"Tokyo?" I repeated. "Wait, younger?" He nodded. "Around my age?" He shook his head.

"No, my parents let me make it through most of elementary school before she came along." He sounded disgruntled.

"And I assume that wasn't cool?" Being the oldest, I could relate to being a little agitated when my sisters came along—but they came along quickly, too quickly for me to enjoy being an only child.

"Eventually, I learned that it was the best thing that happened to me," he laughed, "but it took some time."

The words, "How many kids do you want?" came out of my mouth before I realized what I was asking.

He asked, "You trying to have my babies?" with his lip curved into a crooked smile. The waitress returned with the crab dip, and I let that question hang in the air as he spooned out dip for each of us on the small plates. After I had a mouthful of dip, he reiterated, "Okay, maybe it's too early to commit to having my babies." Then he looked at me with a blank face and asked, "But do you want kids?"

That was a serious question that deserved a thoughtful answer—one I had been thinking about more and more in recent years. The further I was away from my last relationship, I started to think of alternative options, or realities that didn't align with my desire, so when I answered, "Absolutely," there was no doubt in my mind I wanted to have kids. But with who, that was the real question that needed answers.

"How many?" I told him I didn't mind a couple. "Hmmm..." I started to think what if he didn't want kids, and if I'd automatically dismiss him or wait for him to come around, but then he replied, "For sure, a little Jojo, Jo Jr., my twin." I realized he had put as much thought into it as I had. "Sooner than later, I hope." His shoulders hunched, and I started to think about what *that* meant.

The conversation got lighter, and we finished our meals— drinks and dessert, then Joseph asked, "Do you have plans tomorrow?" I shook my head, and he said, "How about you come over to my place, and I show you what I can do in the kitchen?"

"And he cooks?" I smiled widely.

CHAPTER TEN

JOSEPH

"Man, why did you tell that girl you can cook?" Alonzo looked at me with the ball clutched into his side. "Bruh, last cookout we had you burnt the chicken." I shook my head. "Oh, you don't remember that rubbery ass chicken?" He looked to Chris for confirmation. "You remember," he coached him.

Chris wagged his head. "I mean, the chicken was a little tough." Then he gritted his teeth. "And a little salty."

"A little?" Alonzo shouted. "I don't even think you seasoned the chicken. I think you just poured on the salt and thought that was it." Chris had started to laugh until I looked at him.

"Forget you, that was just a bad day," I grumbled.

"A bad day?" Chris repeated then tried to remind me of other meals I may have botched. "You better call Ms. Long and ask her to save the day."

Then Chris had to give his spin on Marcia being bourgeois and not accepting anything less than a perfect meal. "Might be better to go ahead and find a home chef to whip something up for you." Then his eyes grew wide. "Or better yet, order some take-out and plop that shit on a plate."

Alonzo co-signed that idea. "Hell yeah, there you go." He slapped my shoulder. "Don't even have to put in work."

Chris nodded his head. "Sounds like a winning plan right there." I shook my head and grabbed my towel before I left the gym. When I offered to cook, it seemed like a nice plan to be in the house with Marcia. But I forgot about the actual effort of cooking, and although I ate what I cooked, I couldn't completely disagree with Alonzo. My mama hadn't passed on her cooking skills.

"Mama," I sighed when she answered the phone, "I need help."

"What you need, Jojo?" I could hear the wind whipping against the phone and thought she was likely outside in her garden. "Hold on." Then I heard her curse. "These bugs are something else this year." She cursed again, a little louder. "They better not ruin my crop."

"I was hoping you had time today to help me whip up a meal."

I was surprised when she repeated, "Whip up a meal?" Then added, "Like cook you some food?"

"Not exactly." I heard her shuffling around. "I wanted to know if you could come over and walk me through something fairly easy."

"Today?" I didn't understand why she was hesitating. We usually ate a few meals together during the week, most of which she'd cook. "I was going to an event downtown." Then she paused. "Why am I helping you cook a meal?"

"I invited Marcia over." She interrupted me, laughing. "What?"

"You told that girl you can cook, didn't you?" I mumbled my response, but my mama came to my rescue. "Okay, but after you eat you better tell that woman you can't cook worth a damn."

"Wow. Really, Mama?"

"If you could, you wouldn't be calling me, right?" I ignored her and asked if she could send me the ingredients to her stewed chicken and rice. "Oh, you really are trying to impress her, huh?" I heard the door open and shut. "Pulling out your mama's infamous stewed chicken."

"I mean, if I'm going to cook, I might as well impress her." My mama agreed to send me the ingredients and meet me at my house in a couple of hours. "Thank you, Mama." I smiled before hanging up the phone with her.

The plan was working itself out. Until I made it to the grocery store and I could hardly navigate the aisles to find the ingredients. I was standing in the middle of the spice aisle scanning the shelf, when I heard someone whisper, "I'll be damned." I turned around to see a woman whispering into her phone. When our eyes connected, they were vaguely familiar. "Joseph?" she asked.

I narrowed my brows and nodded my head. "Yes."

She moved the phone from her ear. "It's so nice to finally meet you." But I still had no idea who she was. "I'm Nicolette." I shook my head. "Marcia's sister."

"Oh, Nic?" I responded, and she smiled.

"I've heard so much about you, but Marcia has been holding you back. I told her I'd bump into you one day." She winked. "It is a small town, after all." I nodded my head in agreement. I was reminded of that more and more each day since I had moved back home. She glanced into my cart and said, "What are you cooking?"

I proudly responded, "My mama's famous stewed chicken." Then I added, "For your sister."

She cocked her head. "Okay, trying to scoop her up?" She laughed, and I wagged my head. "Keep doing what you're doing, and you might just do that." She smiled and sauntered away. I watched her as she turned the corner of the aisle. Her skin, the same chocolatey brown as her sister, and her eyes a direct copy and paste of the almond shape—but her height and thickness were not comparable. Marcia was a few inches taller, and she was blessed with thickness in all the right places. But I could see what would have Chris damn near about to fight for Nic. She was beautiful.

I grabbed the paprika and made my way to the checkout counter. As the cashier swiped each item, I thought about how the night would go. My mama's meal would definitely be a hit, but I'd have to eventually tell Marcia that I couldn't really throw down in the kitchen.

When I opened the front door, though, the look of excitement on Marcia's face when she took in that first whiff of stewed chicken was worth all the trouble that went into being in the kitchen with my mama. "I thought we could use a little dessert." She held up a pack of cupcakes, and I smiled.

I recognized the sunshine-yellow packaging right away. "From Dickerson's?" I grinned. "Most definitely." Dickerson's was a Rolling Hills staple. The family owned bakery had been around since I was a kid and was likely being run by some descendant of the Mrs. Dickerson herself. "Who is baking these days anyway?"

I looked back at Marcia's face as I made my way to the kitchen. "Good question." She laughed. "I guess Mrs. Dickerson would be a little too old to be still in the kitchen, huh?" She cocked her head. "She must have done a great job writing down those recipes." She peered around the kitchen. "Because I certainly can't tell that they aren't still her magnificent creations." I peeked inside the box to take inventory of which cupcakes she brought. "I got a variety just in case." I smiled and nodded.

"They'll be a perfect ending to this meal." I opened the lid of the pot and stirred the chicken as my mama told me to do before she left. She warned me to not let the grease settle on top. I looked into the pot, not sure what to expect but stirred anyway. "Ready to eat?"

"If it tastes anything like it smells, absolutely." She placed her purse on the couch then joined me in the kitchen. "Can I help?" I shook my head. "Okay," she said before leaving me to it in the kitchen.

I brought a bottle of wine and two glasses to the table first. "Red wine?" I said, pulling the cork out.

She took a sip and said, "I'm not one to get excited about food." She looked down at her glass as she swirled the wine around. "But you have me over here excited to taste what's in that pot." She looked toward the kitchen. I turned away and laughed.

With both plates prepared, I carried them slowly to the table. "Stewed chicken." I placed a plate in front of her. "With mixed vegetables on the side."

She looked over her plate and nodded slowly before she looked across the table at me. "This smells amazing, and looks really good." She picked up her fork and cut a small piece of chicken, scooped up some rice, and slowly pulled it all off into her mouth in a single bite. Her eyes widened as she chewed. "Wow."

I took a bite of my own, and I was glad it tasted just like I remembered growing up. My mom joked that I would pull out one of her classic meals to cook for a woman. The look on Marcia's face was everything I could have hoped for, and more. "I'm glad you like it." She continued eating then cocked her head. "What's that about?" I asked, putting my fork down.

"Nic told me she saw you at the store today." I nodded my head. "On the seasoning aisle." I nodded again.

"Yes, grabbing all the ingredients." I stared at her before noting, "I'm not sure how she recognized me actually."

She didn't respond to that, but she said, "She mentioned you looked a little lost in the grocery store."

"Lost?" I asked defensively. "How is one supposed to look in the grocery store?"

Then she confessed, "I'm not sure because," she shrugged, "I don't cook." I wasn't surprised, though. She ate a lot of salad, and probably didn't spend a lot of time in the kitchen.

"Oh," I responded before announcing, "Okay, so this is my mom's recipe."

She took another bite then said, "Seems about right." But then I explained how she came over to help me prepare it. "Wait, you had Mama Long in the kitchen helping you cook?" Her nose scrunched up. "For me?" I nodded my head. "How'd she feel about that? I haven't even met the woman yet and I'll already be on her shit list." She laughed.

I shook my head. "No, she seemed to enjoy being in the kitchen with me, bossing me around."

Marcia's eyes narrowed. "And you volunteered to cook knowing you can't cook, why?" She grabbed her glass of wine and took a sip as I thought about that question honestly.

"How else could I invite you over to my place?" I adjusted in my seat. "Certainly couldn't ask you over to *Netflix and Chill*."

"You got that right," she quickly responded. "But..." She looked around then back to me. "You could have ordered food." She laughed. "You know I have no problems ordering food." I hadn't thought about it, but our first night together she had ordered food.

"Could have." Then I reached across the table for her hand. "But nothing beats a home-cooked meal."

"And I appreciate you for taking the effort. You'll have to spend more time in the kitchen with your mom if this is the result." She smiled and looked down at the food. "Now I'm trying to figure out how to get on your mama's Sunday invite list." My eyes narrowed. "Oh, I know her Sunday dinners have to be ridiculous." She laughed.

I hunched my shoulders. "Got plans tomorrow?" I asked before thinking about how my mama would curse me out for inviting her to Sunday dinner with short notice.

Marcia must have felt the same when she reiterated, "Tomorrow?" She shook her head. "Didn't I just say I'm on Mama's shit list?" She laughed. "I don't know about your mother, but mine would kill me if I had a spontaneous dinner guest."

"Spontaneous dinner guest?" I repeated. "Sounds like I should be trying to get on your mama's Sunday invite list." I winked.

For the first time ever, I heard her confidence wane. When she said, "Oh no, I'm not sure you're ready to meet my mother." Her gaze went away from me, and she pulled her hand away to grab her wine glass.

"You okay?" I asked.

"It's just that my mother is strictly business, even when she's at home. Dinner with her is like," she paused, "it's just not all that comfortable."

"Got it." I let her slide because she looked more and more uncomfortable sitting across from me. "Maybe we'll stick to dinner with each other for a while." She smiled.

"I like that idea." Then she laughed. "But I'm not going to even attempt to cook for you."

My mouth dropped. "Damn, you can't even throw a sandwich together for your man?"

Her eyes widened, and before I could retract any of my words, she was replying, "My man?" Her head dipped to the side. "How would you feel if you were my man, but I never cooked?"

"We talking like never ever?" She nodded her head. "Like not even Sunday dinners for the kids?"

"Kids?" she blurted.

"Yeah, you know when we have those few kids—back to back —they will need to eat too." I couldn't tell if she was contemplating cooking or the kids, or maybe my sudden approach of attaching her to me. "Maybe we should take some cooking lessons."

She gritted her teeth but then nodded her head. "Maybe."

CHAPTER ELEVEN

MARCIA

"Ready for dessert?" I asked as I lay my fork on the plate. Joseph stood from the table ready to grab the plates, but I insisted, "No, let me." Then I laughed. "The least I can do since I didn't cook or even make the dessert." The thought of doing either didn't make me feel as awkward as I imagined. Cooking for a family would probably be necessary. Even my mama, the business mogul, found time to cook us a home-cooked meal a few nights a week. "Which cupcake would you like?" I asked, not realizing Joseph was right behind me.

"I'll take the"—he kissed the back of my neck—"chocolate with chocolate frosting." I opened the box, trying to remember if I even bought a chocolate cupcake.

Searching for it, I responded, "I didn't get chocolate."

I felt his lips on me again, before he whispered, "Oh, I know," in my ear. "How about we save *that* dessert for later." His arms went to my sides, and I was caged in, my back still turned to him. With my rule out the door, I had to agree. I wanted a taste of him more than any cupcake in that box.

"Only if I don't fill you up," I said, turning to face him. Our eyes connected, and as he leaned into me, mine closed softly. I could still taste the red wine on his lips, and as his tongue entered into my mouth, I knew I was losing myself to him.

His arms left my sides and I felt his hands on my waist, then my back, and we were even closer. Then he pulled away and looked down at me. "Can I take you to my room?"

I teased, "Dessert in bed? That might get messy."

He quickly replied, "I hope so." He reached for my hand and I followed him through the kitchen, down the hall, into his bedroom. As much as I wanted to look around and see how he was living, Joseph had all my attention when he started pulling his shirt over his head in front of me.

My high-waisted pants and crop top couldn't get out of the way fast enough. I pulled at the hem of my pants, trying to unbutton each tightly wound button, before I sighed. "Damn," I whispered.

"At least they are cute." Joseph smiled at me then offered, "Let me help you." He grabbed my hands, moving them aside, before he carefully unbuttoned each button of my pants. "If I were willing to bet, looks like you were trying to keep your pants on tonight." I looked up at him and shook my head because that couldn't have been further from the truth. As my pants slid down my legs, I stood there in my top and panties as he took a step back and gazed at me. In one quick gesture, his pants were on the floor beside him. "Once you cross that line it's hard to go back, right?" he asked as he came closer. I felt his warm hands on my bare skin, and it felt like my body was shivering.

"Right," I whispered as I tugged my shirt over my head. "No turning back." Before I could finish my sentence, I felt his lips on mine, his tongue slowly gliding into my mouth. "Ehm," I mumbled between kisses.

His finger traced the lining of my lace panties, and I felt my nerves tingling all over my body. From the top of my head down to the tip of my toes, my body was buzzing. Then he dipped a finger beneath the lace, and my head fell back. His mouth went to my neck and I was very much ready to lie down and let him do whatever it was he wanted to do with me, as long as the vibrations didn't stop.

But he didn't. He didn't lay me across the bed. He didn't continue his trail of kisses down my body. His finger slipped out of my panties, and my eyes jolted open. "What happened?" I asked as I tried to catch my breath.

"Last time I was a little rushed." Even in the darkness his features were pronounced—his eyes were barely open, and his mouth lacked the grin I was growing to adore. "Tonight, do I have your permission to take my time?" Then I saw his mouth creep into a smile as I nodded my head slowly in response. "Good," he whispered as his mouth went back to mine and his hands softly caressed my skin. "Lay down," he ordered as he backed away. "I'll be right back." I lay across his bed but I watched, waiting for his return.

When he said he wanted to take his time, I didn't know what to expect, but when he returned and asked, "Can you flip over for me." I hesitated. With a small laugh, he assured me, "Trust me, you'll enjoy this."

I turned onto my stomach but looked over my shoulder, just in case. When I saw a burning candle, I said, "Wait, what are you doing with that?"

Then oil dripped down the middle of my back, and I rested my head against the pillow when his hands followed behind it, working my back between his fingers in small circles. My mouth fell open as he worked out kinks I think even my masseuse may have missed. There was more oil, and more massaging, and when he worked his way down my legs, I felt the tingling in my body start up again. I had to concentrate to keep myself from squirming. I felt his hands on my feet and I was glad I never missed a trip to the nail salon.

I heard a soft hum coming from him as he massaged the sole of my foot. "You are gorgeous from the top of your head to the bottom of your feet." I didn't know how to respond, and I smiled, although with my head buried into the pillow he couldn't see it.

Between the compliments and the massaging, I was feeling a tingling somewhere else—in my chest. Thankfully, his kisses distracted me from that feeling, because there was no way after several dates I was feeling *that*.

After a kiss on my ankle, he instructed me to flip over again, and this time I did it with no hesitation. "Marcia," he said softly as his hands made their way to my thighs, "I don't know what you are doing to me." At least the feeling was mutual.

"Nothing more than what you are doing to me." My eyes gently opened, and his head dipped down and back up again. "More nights like these and you may not be able to get rid of me."

"If that's a promise..." He kissed the hem of my panties. "I can pencil you in." I didn't reply, I couldn't reply, because after that he pulled them down and ran his tongue through the folds of my pussy, and thoughts were incomprehensible. "Yeah, I can definitely pencil you in," he said between licks.

My body relaxed as he took his time, exploring the intricacies between my thighs. All the while his hands roamed and massaged— my stomach, my legs, and even down to my feet when he placed them on his shoulders, spreading my legs even wider. I lay wide open with his head between my legs, my body reaching the edge of ecstasy.

Then his fingers dipped in, giving his tongue a well-deserved break. But the way he massaged my clit almost sent me over, and he must have felt my body begin to pulse because he pulled back and warned, "Not yet."

I opened my eyes slightly, and his were on me along with a

smirk on his face. He looked sexy as fuck, just like that. "I don't know how much longer I can hold on," I said with a whimper.

"I won't make you wait long," he said before reaching up to intertwine our fingers. I shut my eyes as he went back to business, and my body picked up right where he left off, one step off the edge. His tongue flicked across my clit a few times, and that was it. I took the step off the edge, and I went crashing into bliss. He climbed off the bed as I lay there motionless—breathless. Eyes closed, I could only hear him moving around the room.

I listened as he made his way back to the bed, and heard when he ripped the condom wrapper open, as he took a breath, then I felt his knee beside me as he climbed back onto the bed. I took a deep breath when I felt him hovering over me.

His lips came crashing down just as I felt him enter me. My hands were moving, grasping, all over his wide back. He had me boxed in between his strong arms, one on each side of my head as he worked his thrust, in and out. Our kisses continued, erratically, until he slowed his pace and pulled his lips from mine. He trailed kisses down my neck and across my chest, until he took a nipple into his mouth and sucked it like a lollipop. Not even our first time—the time that broke my long dry spell—did I feel as much pleasure.

From the top of my head where I felt secure between his arms, to the tips of my nipples where the sensation of his warm mouth had my eyes clenched closed, to the pulsing of my pussy where he entered me deeply, on down to my toes that were curling from the many sensations throughout my body. I could have easily been floating on a cloud and I wouldn't have known the difference.

His hand reached between us, and I felt his finger searching around until it made contact with my clit and, "Oh my gawd," I squealed. He was rubbing, still while his dick was going in, and out, then he bit down on my nipple and I just lost it. I turned my head into the pillow and allowed it to suffocate my loud moans.

"You good?" he asked between thrusts. I couldn't respond, so he slowed and repeated himself, "For real, you good?"

I turned my head until I saw his eyes looking down at me, and I whispered, "Yeah."

He took that as ammunition to whatever was driving him, and he went from gently coaxing me into ecstasy to fucking me into delirium. My eyes widened and I sucked in a breath as I felt my body finally give in. My hand went to his chest, and I traced down to his pelvis area. "Wait," I warned, as he moved from on top of me.

"Don't worry," he laughed, "we have all night."

CHAPTER TWELVE

JOSEPH

I'm not one to cancel plans, ever. But when an emergency happened at work, I had no choice but to cancel my plans with Marcia. Then the next day when my mama called for help, I knew I was the only one who could be there for her.

"Tell me again." I looked at my mama then to Alonzo, who was on the opposite side of the couch directing it out of the house. "Why we had to move this furniture *today*."

My mama was ignoring me and instead, asked Alonzo, "If your mama cooked for you on the regular, even for one of your dates, then was the reason for your little girlfriend, would you have a problem helping her out when she needed?" She stood near the doorway watching as we tried to maneuver the oversized couch through the door.

"No, ma'am, I sure wouldn't," Alonzo said as he smirked. "I'd just show up whenever she needed me, no questions asked."

My mama had known Alonzo since he was a little kid, coming to our house after school, most weekends, he even rode with us to many of our youth basketball games. Then I left for college, and Alonzo made sure my parents never needed anything. In the past year, he had been instrumental with helping my mama while I was preparing myself to move back to Rolling Hills. To say he was like the brother I never had, would be an understatement.

But the way he curved me on the regular for my mama, had me feeling some type of way. "You know you are going to get the same meal after we finish whether you agree or not, right?" We stepped down the set of stairs leading from the house into the garage.

As we sat the couch down to the side of the garage, Alonzo said, "I mean, but it's true." I crossed my arms across my chest. "It's the least I could do, right?"

I smacked my lips. "Man, whatever." I laughed, knowing that Alonzo was about that bullshit, because there were a few times when his mama asked for similar favors and I ended up on the other end of a phone call because she couldn't, 'locate her son.' "Like the last time your mama needed help and she called me to hang those pictures."

"She didn't need help with that." Then he paused and cocked his head. "But at least you had picture-hanging skills ready to use when you really did need them." Alonzo had plopped himself down onto the couch, leaning back all comfortable. "Just think, if you didn't have that as an excuse to get over to Marcia's house."

I looked around, back and forth from the garage door to the couch. "Excuse?" I shook my head. "I didn't need an excuse."

Alonzo leaned forward on the couch. "Oh, 'cause she was just willing to kick it with you." He waited for me but didn't get a response. "Because I thought she didn't want anything to do with your ass until after those pictures were hung, then just like that"—he snapped his finger—"she was all over you." He put his hand in the air. "Wait a minute, now that I think about it..." He slowly nodded his head. "Remind me to always be available for my mama if she needs work done around the house."

"Oh." I narrowed my eyes. "You just don't want someone creeping with your mama." I laughed as Alonzo grabbed a pillow and tried to throw it at me.

"If you didn't feel the same way, you wouldn't have been so quick to be up over here when Ms. Long called." He cocked his head, and I laughed it off as I walked back into the house, waiting for my mama to bark out more instructions.

"I think that's it," she said as she glanced around the now empty living room.

I understood my mama wanting to change up the place. After nearly a decade with the same furniture, it was definitely time, but I knew that was the furniture we had when Pops was around, so I asked, "You okay?" as she stood in the middle of the living room.

She nodded her head slowly and replied, "I am, Jojo." She looked at Alonzo then back to me. "I am. Many thanks to both of you for dropping everything to get it done."

I hesitated but asked anyway, "When is the new furniture coming?" She told me the delivery was scheduled to arrive the next day. "And they will set it up for you?" She nodded her head, and I was a little relieved. "The folks picking up that furniture will be here soon?" I stopped and let her reply.

"Yes. But it's fine, I'll be okay," she responded, as I stood with my arms across my chest, shaking my head.

"No, I'll stick around." I went to tap Alonzo on his back, but he declined me trying to dismiss him. "I'm good, bruh."

He shook his head. "I don't have anywhere else to be right now," he said confidently, and I wished I could repeat the same, but I did have somewhere to be. Or at least I was supposed to be. I was supposed to be with Marcia making up for the night before when I had to cancel on her.

"Okay." I looked to my mama and rubbed my belly. "Any food in there?" She pulled out leftovers from the fridge, and I was wondering why she had so many. "Who you been cooking for?" I asked as I watched her pull out the last container from the fridge. Even when I did come by her place a few nights a week she didn't cook all that food.

Alonzo grabbed a plate and started piling food on top, when he stopped and smirked. "That's my business," my mama said sternly as she wiped the counter.

The furniture moving, the meals she was cooking, I blurted, "Mama, you got some man coming over here?" I narrowed my eyes. "What?" I said when she couldn't hide the wide grin on her face.

"You have to live your life, and I can't just sit around counting down the days till you or your sister give me grandkids."

Then I thought about my little sister and blurted, "Does she know? Does Tanya know?"

My mom's eyes widened, then she shrugged. "Maybe. Why?" I had more questions, but my mama finally retorted, "Listen, when the time is right I'll let you know exactly who he is, and I'll introduce you to him."

I sat at the table as I spooned some of my favorite dishes into my mouth—candied yams, stewed chicken, collard greens. Then I said, "And you cooked him your holiday mac and cheese." I threw my hands up, "In the middle of summer?"

Alonzo and my mama both laughed. "It is good, Ms. Long." Alonzo piled on as he sat beside me shoveling food into his mouth.

But before we could say any more, there was a knock at the door and my mama announced, "Must be the people for the furniture."

Alonzo leaned into me and said, "Guess it was your mama we

should have been worried about." I shook my head and put my fork down.

"This some bullshit," I said as I made my way to the garage. Alonzo was close behind and tried to convince me it was good for her to be moving on. "My dad has only been gone a year." Then I added, "If that."

We stood in the garage waiting for the Bubba Gump-looking dudes to grab the two couches and the tables from the garage, then load them into their truck. "We appreciate this, Ms. Long." I looked to Alonzo, who had his head cocked.

"They know her?" he said before looking back at the two guys. Of course, they would have known her name if they were getting furniture from her, but the way they said her name, laughed, and talked with her after the furniture was loaded onto the truck, was more familiar than just a casual pick up.

"That's why she was okay with being here alone." I shook my head as they drove off and my mama walked back to the two of us. "Mama, you know them?" I asked as I followed behind her.

"Did you two finish up your food?" She ignored my entire question. "I know you had plans, and I don't want to ruin your *entire* night."

Besides my plans being postponed, my mama having a dude fucked my night all the way up. "It's cool, I might as well stick around here," I said firmly. She tried to encourage me to leave, but that shit wasn't happening. I was on watch for this old man who thought he found him something new. "Yeah," I looked to Alonzo and affirmed, "I'll see you on Monday. I'm just going to make myself comfortable for a while."

He laughed then highlighted, "With no furniture." Then he laughed, too hard, after he added, "Good luck with that." He leaned into my mama and said loudly, "You do you, Ms. Long."

I shoved him out the door, abruptly cutting off any response my mom was trying to give him.

CHAPTER THIRTEEN

MARCIA

Retail therapy wasn't easy in a small town. I had already spent my day in the boutique trying on all of their newest additions. Then proceeding to buy a few options for what I thought would have been a make-up date from the night before. But as each text Joseph sent came in, I was starting to doubt my plans for the night, again.

Instead, I changed into a pair of sweats, had my hair pulled into a ponytail, and my laptop open beside me. Different tabs open, I didn't have anything in mind to buy, but I needed something to keep me from incessantly checking my phone.

Then my phone rang, and it made me jump—half scaring me, then exciting me. But I saw my sister's name flash across the screen and I grumbled. I told them about my cancelled plans the night prior, but hadn't told them my Saturday night was also looking like trash. I tried to disguise the disappointment in my voice when I answered, "Hello," sounding extra chipper.

"Are you about to leave?" Before I could respond, Liv was already blurting, "Can I borrow that yellow dress?"

I squinted before I slowly responded, "You mean the one I

haven't worn yet?" She agreed, but I shut that shit down with the quickness. "Hell no."

She began to try to negotiate with me. When she offered, "I'll buy you lunch Monday *and* Tuesday." I laughed at the offer, and she said, "Right, food doesn't win with you." She was half right, up against my wardrobe it would never win. "How about a one-hour massage next weekend?"

She was on to something with that offer because I loved a good pampering session. I looked down at my bare feet and said, "Throw in a pedicure and you can come pick it up." She grumbled about the cost being pricier than the dress, and I snapped, "That's a negative. Besides that..." I stopped to think about why she needed a last-minute dress, one she couldn't find in her own damn closet. "Wait, what do you need the yellow dress for anyway?" Liv's closet was pretty impressive, she wasn't on my level yet, but she was getting there. No doubt she didn't have something nearly as cute as the yellow dress I found at the boutique months ago. I was holding for the right night out, maybe a date with Joseph. Then the thought of him standing me up had me in my feelings again.

So much so, I almost missed when Liv mumbled, "I have a date."

"A date, with who?" I was intrigued because her luck with men wasn't any better than mine. Then I sensed she was hesitating. "Liv?" I asked sternly. Out of all my mother's children, Liv was the adventurous one, and likely to be doing some shit she shouldn't be doing.

"Okay," she finally blurted, "I don't exactly have a date." I pulled the phone closer to my ear to hear what crazy story she was about to tell me—after all, I didn't have anywhere to be, and nothing but time to waste.

"Actually, if you didn't have plans, I'd invite you out." I grumbled because technically I didn't have plans, and I was contemplating letting her know. Then she explained, "Speed Dating."

"Speed Dating?" I repeated. Then came her explanation, and as she explained the concept that was supposedly for black professionals only, I considered the idea more. Although I wasn't into dating apps, or responding to men hopping in my DMs, I wanted to find love the old fashioned way—bumping into a sexy ass man in the grocery store, in church, somewhere completely random—I was considering going just for the hell of it.

"I'll go." But that meant I'd have to get off the couch and into an outfit.

"You'll go?" Her tone pitched. "Where is Joseph? And," she quickly added in, "can I still borrow the dress?"

I purposely ignored her question about Joseph, and told her, "Yes, you can borrow it. What time does it start?" I was already moving from the living room to my closet. I pulled the yellow dress and draped it over the bed. Then I slushed through my clothes racks as she tried to pry about Joseph. "You'll be here soon?"

She didn't complain too much about me ignoring her questions. Pretty sure she wasn't even excited about me going to the event, but more so about me still letting her borrow my dress. "I'll be there in twenty," she promised. Before she hung up, she suggested, "Might as well make this a Mercy Girls Night Out."

I shrugged, although she couldn't see me, and I said, "Might as well." Liv and Nic were at my house as promised, but later than expected. I had already found an orange, flowing dress, a pair of heels, and showered by the time they knocked on the door. I went to the door with my makeup brush in hand. "And don't think I didn't realize you ignored my question about my future brother-in-law," Liv hummed before she was completely in the house.

I hurried back to the bathroom and shouted, "Dress is on the bed," over my shoulder as I walked away. Thankful for the break away from checking my phone, I didn't want to start thinking about why Joseph cancelled Friday night, then didn't even call to cancel Saturday night. The last I heard, he was still *busy*. "Dammit," I whispered to myself in the mirror. I didn't want to think about his ass and how he, 'got the milk for free,' as my mama used to warn us when we were in college.

Liv walked into the bathroom behind me with a smirk on her face. "I think this one actually looks even better on my complexion." She twirled and I looked up to see her in the orange dress I picked out for myself. Her doing as she pleased didn't surprise me, so I couldn't even be mad that she grabbed my dress. It was a part of her M.O., but the fact the orange did look fucking fantastic on her skin, had me a little peeved.

I rolled my eyes and said, "And you better snag a man tonight." She smiled and kissed my cheek.

"Because you aren't actually trying to snag one, are you?" She peered at me through the mirror and I shrugged. "Oh shit." She dashed out of the bathroom, and all I could hear was loud banter between her and Nic in the living room. Then before I could even think about what I could say in response, Nic had busted in the bathroom.

"That nigga," she said with too much bass in her voice. "What'd he do already?"

I laughed and said, "He cancelled our date." She shook her head. "Last night and tonight."

"Just when I thought you found a good gone." She sucked her teeth. "Men just can't help but be fuck boys." She patted my shoulder and said, "Don't worry, this speed dating might just be your lucky night." She winked.

And if she meant—a room full of fine ass men—lucky, then she was right. We walked into the lounge and were greeted by the host, but as I stood listening to instructions, I glanced around the room and my mouth dropped. "Who knew all this was right next door to Rolling Hills?" Nic whispered into my ear. "They been holding out on us over here in *Dear Creek*." She stepped back and mumbled, "Dear Motherfucking Creek."

"Okay, we are going to post up over here, side-by-side." Liv laughed. "They have to at least want one of the Mercy Sisters."

Nic trailed behind but said, "Or all of 'em." I laughed, but tried not to bring too much attention to us before we could make it to our seats. It wasn't long after we sat down that the event started. Each of us had a table to ourselves, and the men were circulating the room.

The first guy that sat across from me, he was cute, but had a boyish style that wasn't as appealing. When he asked, "Do you like clubbing?" I was glad he was quickly on to the next person.

"Ugh," Liv whispered as her guy moved on. "Okay, maybe these guys don't have the energy I need in my life."

The next guy sat across from me, and he looked old enough to be my daddy. In fact, he may have been one of my daddy's friends. When he asked, "Are you Ferg's daughter?" I scrunched my nose and nodded my head.

"I am," I said confidently. "Are you a friend of his?" He laughed, a little nervously, and I said, "Cool," as he winked and stood to leave. "What the hell?" I whispered more to myself than to anyone listening.

"Not what you were expecting?" I heard the guy standing near my table say before my eyes met his. And damn. His smooth, dark skin served as a backdrop to his beautiful, white smile and deep-brown eyes. "You were definitely worth my trip to this small town."

Intrigued, I asked, "Oh yeah? What big city did you travel from?" He sat across from me and wiped his thick hand across the stubble around his jaw.

"Sur." His voice was even deeper than when he first spoke. I found myself leaning into him, mesmerized by the baritone.

Sur was the city Rolling Hills and Dear Creek surrounded. I wouldn't consider it a *big city* by any stretch of the imagination, but it was more city than where we were. "Oh, okay." He smiled and I asked, "And what do you do in Sur?"

The response he gave was unexpected, not that a sexy ass black man couldn't be that and educated, but I think his response had my panties dripping. "I've always loved kids, so becoming a pediatrician seemed like a smooth move." And he loved kids— might as well have painted my face with the heart eyes emoji. "What about you?" He looked around as other men were rotating, but he didn't budge. "This may be risky, but do you mind joining me at the bar?"

My eyes widened slightly because that wasn't a part of the rules. Then, of course, there was the man back in Rolling Hills— who stood me up, twice. "Sure." I looked to my right and announced to Nic, "I'm going over to the bar with..."

"Hold up, you leaving the game?" Liv shouted. "I don't think that's how it works."

Nic had her own input to add, "And you don't even know his name." Her eyes traveled his body, then she said, "But I don't even blame you, go on with your nameless lover."

The man who extended the invite seemed to be enjoying the banter between my sisters. "I take it you all came here together?" he asked with a hitched brow. When I nodded, he explained, "Well, I hope I'm not ruining your night." He looked to Liv and Nic. "Was just hoping we could take more time than the rotation allowed." He moved a hand to my lower back, and I tried not to react to his touch as he offered, "And my name is Boris."

Nic quickly replied, "And you look like a Boris." I could hear him chuckle. "Alright, we'll catch up with you after this is all over." She looked at him then warned, "Don't think she's going to run off with you to the bathroom and fuck you senseless."

"Whoa." His hand slipped from my back. "Not like that at all."

Nic winked and offered, "Just joking," then she looked to her side as a guy was approaching her table, "unless you wanted to, then..." And she shrugged as I took the guy standing in front of us as an opportunity to leave.

"She was animated," Boris said as we approached the bar. "But good friends are always overprotective." He paused then added, "I guess." I took the opportunity to let him know Nic and Liv were my sisters. As I sat beside him, I watched as his face formed into a few different forms. "Oh, I guess I do see the resemblance actually."

I smiled because the resemblance wasn't obvious. We each had our own traits that we inherited from our parents, combining to make three distinct women. Not to mention we all had a different style, so not many could guess that we were sisters.

"And, of the three, where do you fall in the lineup?" Because we were also close in age, telling who was the oldest, or youngest, wasn't always easy either.

"The oldest." He smiled. When he guessed that Nic was the middle child, I had to laugh. "Can you tell?" He nodded his head. The bartender approached and informed us of the drink specials. "I'll have the pineapple crush." I looked to Boris, who was staring at me before he ordered a gin and tonic.

"So, whose idea was it to come to the speed dating?" he asked after the bartender placed my drink in front of me.

I thought back to the start of my day—and how I was preparing to be on a date with Joseph. Then how disappointed I was when he texted to tell me something came up, again. "It was the youngest's idea," I responded, thinking about Liv and her request to wear my dress. Then I cocked my head slightly. "And what about you? What made you come to Dear Creek for an event like this?" I teased, "Ran out of potential women in Sur?"

"This will sound a little bizarre." He looked back to the area where the daters were seated. "But the organizer is one of my patient's mother."

I shrugged. "I guess that doesn't sound too weird." I thought about him in his element, and how sexy he had to look with a white coat on. Then he explained that she first tried to ask him out on a date. "Oh, well, that turns an innocent invite into an extremely awkward situation." I wondered how that conversation transpired. Then I snaked my neck around to the lady who had given us directions when we first arrived.

"Extremely awkward." He shook his head. "I definitely don't make it a habit to date my patient's mothers." He smirked. "Grandmothers or aunties." I laughed, but his face remained unfazed. "There have been a few."

"I mean—sexy, educated, a little bit of money, maybe." Then after I gassed him up, I said, "And single."

"Emphasis on little." His nose crinkled. "But wait, that doesn't help my case here." He smiled. "We'll disregard that, and I won't remind myself how expensive medical school was."

"I bet. More money, more problems." He smiled at that reference and nodded his head. We continued chatting about school, our cities, and I even learned he was not from the area originally. "Maryland?"

"I know, a long way from home." He was explaining what brought him to the West Coast when Nic and Liv appeared beside me. "Any luck?" he asked the two of them as they ordered a drink.

Nic huffed and Liv laughed. "A little," Liv responded, but Nic rolled her eyes.

Boris was going back and forth with them when I felt my phone vibrate a few times. I was going to ignore it till it continued. I looked down and saw Joseph's name flashing on the screen. "Excuse me for a minute," I said as I stepped away from the bar.

"Hey," he said calmly.

"Hey?" I started to tell him exactly how I felt about being stood up, not once, but twice, but I heard the strain in his voice.

"I apologize for missing our date, again." I could hear him yawn. "My mom needed some help moving furniture."

"And it had to be moved today? All day? Is she moving out of the house?" I asked, trying to justify his excuse.

"Just the living room furniture." Then he explained, "And I think she has a man."

I laughed until I realized he was seriously put off by it. "Is that why you sound all caught up in your feelings?" I looked over to the bar and Boris was looking over his shoulder, and smiled when our gazes connected.

He tried to deny feeling some type of way. "But I am tired, I won't ask to have more of your time, especially not after these past two days failed, but—" Before he could continue, I cut him off.

"Can I call you back? I'm actually out right now."

"Oh, yeah." He paused. "Sure, call me back whenever you are free."

I went back to the bar, beside Boris and my sisters, who were still going back and forth about their lack of a date.

"Speaking of dates," Boris chimed in, "would you mind if I took you out on a date?" I looked beside me to Nic and Liv, whose eyes were wide. Nic nodded her head.

"That would be nice," I responded honestly.

After we exchanged numbers, I walked out of the restaurant with Nic and Liv bickering behind me. "Isn't that some shit?" Nic finally said when we were in front of Liv's car. "You already have a man, and you are out here snatching up more." She frowned. "Just greedy."

"Step your game up, sis," I teased. "If you were on it, there wouldn't be any men out here for me to snatch up."

"Well damn," Nic said with a side eye. We rode back to Rolling Hills, laughing at the different guys we met—most who were nice looking but lacked any type of substance. "Then had the nerve to be out here asking if I had goals," Nic elaborated from the back seat.

But as she and Liv went on about the next couple of guys, I was left thinking about the two I had and whether letting Boris take me on a date would be a good idea. After all, other than standing me up, twice, Joseph had a lot going for him. Up until then, I wouldn't have even considered dating anyone else. "Do you?" I heard Liv speaking, but thought she and Nic were still going back and forth until she said, "Wow, where are you right now?"

I looked to my side and saw her glancing at me. "Hey, keep your eyes on the road," I warned. "Were you talking to me?"

"Yeah," Nic chimed in from the back seat. "Trying to see if you have food at your house or if we need to stop." As if going to either of their houses wasn't even an option.

I shrugged. "Doubtful." Liv offered to order food to be delivered, and although I was torn, and could use some advice, I knew better. My sisters would just tell me that I was being crazy for even thinking about not going on a date with Boris.

By the time Liv pulled into my parking garage, I had convinced myself that one date wouldn't hurt anything.

CHAPTER FOURTEEN

JOSEPH

When Marcia told me she was out, and hurried me off the phone, I felt some type of way. I spent the rest of the night pacing my mom's kitchen until she finally asked, "What is wrong with you, boy?"

"I was supposed to be out with Marcia tonight."

My mama gave me a side eye and shook her head. "Yet, you are over here worried about me and mine."

Then she went on to remind me that she was out there living her own life because I needed to be living mine.

It was her subtle reminder, "Don't slip up and stop doing what you were doing to get her." When I tried to argue that wasn't the case, she cocked her head and without saying a word, I was reminded of my ex.

The ex who had to 'explore her options,' because she claimed I wasn't pursuing her anymore. *Bullshit.*

But I heard my mama loud and clear. I left her house determined to ensure Marcia knew exactly how I felt. That next day, I called her to set up another date, but wasn't surprised when she was too busy for me. I didn't let that discourage me though. I called her every day for a week just to talk—then as the weekend came close, I asked her out again. Instead of agreeing to go out with me, though, she offered, "How about you attend Sunday dinner with me at my parents' house?"

I was shocked by her offer but didn't hesitate to reply, "Sure."

"Great, it starts at five, and we should leave here around three thirty."

"Three thirty, I'll be at your house." Instead of letting her rush me off the phone, I should have asked her what I should wear. I spent the weekend leading up to the dinner thinking about it. Sunday dinners with my mama were super casual, but something was telling me Sunday dinner at the Mercy house would be anything but casual.

I combed my closet for options—I didn't want to be over-dressed, and not too casual. So I ruled out my Polo shirts and slacks. I finally decided a button up and jeans with a pair of loafers instead of my sneakers would have to do.

Three twenty-nine, I was knocking on Marcia's door. And when she opened, I couldn't contain the smile that creeped up on my face. "Damn, it's been a minute." I opened my arms, and she hesitated before walking into them. "You good?" I asked.

She wasn't looking at me, instead she was doing everything but looking at me. "Yeah," she muttered, "I'm good." Then she walked to the kitchen and grabbed her purse. "I'm ready," she said, closing the door behind her.

She walked out a few steps ahead of me and I was able to watch her flowing pink dress trail behind her. She was gorgeous, and definitely not casual. I was glad I decided on the button down, but I was second-guessing the jeans.

"I should have asked..." She turned over her shoulder. "What I should wear to dinner."

Her eyes narrowed and her nose crinkled. "You look good." Finally, a smile appeared on her face. "Real good, actually."

If it weren't for the time that had elapsed between us, I would have wrapped her in my arms and kissed her. But I had time to work back up to that, I hoped. "What have you been up to?" I asked, thinking it was a simple enough question.

"Ugh," she stammered, "you know," she poked her finger at the elevator button, "not much, I guess."

Maybe she was still pissed about me cancelling on her. I had apologized a couple of times, but I took the elevator time to apologize in person. "Again, I apologize for last weekend. I should have communicated better."

Her eyes looked up to mine, and a small smile crept up on her face. "You know, you apologized already." She smirked. "A couple of times."

I nodded my head. "I did." I reached for her hand and she let me take it. "But not in person." My thumb rubbed across the back of her hand. "Someone has been too busy for me to see in person," I joked, kinda.

The doors opened and she walked out ahead of me. When we crossed the elevator, it was as if the conversation we were having stayed behind. She changed topics to her family, maybe in a way to prepare me. "My dad will likely drill you." Then she laughed, "But he's just a big teddy bear."

"To you." I raised my brows and she laughed.

She went on to tell me about her mother, but she didn't have to tell me much because I had met the matriarch at the mentor event. "I think your mom already likes me." I reminded her she was the reason I was knocking at her door unexpectedly.

"Right," she mumbled. Then her eyes widened. "She doesn't exactly know that we've been hanging out."

Hanging out. I don't know if I would have described what we were doing as hanging out. Maybe dating at the minimum. But in my eyes, we were working on a relationship. I let that ride as she continued to tell me, "I didn't want her taking credit for us. Or thinking I needed her to intervene in my life."

"Okay." I opened the passenger door for her. When I climbed in, I asked, "And now what?"

She looked out of the window as I pulled out of the parking garage, and by the time we made it to the first traffic light, she answered, "I don't know."

"Okay." I tapped my fingers across the steering wheel. Questions were swirling, but instead of letting them pour out, I just took her guidance as we navigated through the town. By the time we made it to the edge of town, the space between houses was no longer walking distance, and the nearest store was too far away to spot. I had been to the outskirts of Rolling Hills, but not often. Even my parents' house was within the city limits. "How much farther?" I asked.

Marcia kinda chuckled and answered, "Only a few more miles." Then she turned to me and said, "I know, it's bad enough that we live in Rolling Hills, but they live in no man's land."

I had to agree. "Yeah, this is out here." Then she explained that her dad imagined all his kids returning home and building homes nearby. "Like next door?"

"Yeah." Her nose crinkled. "I don't know about all that." Then she said, "Take the next right."

I made the right but pointed out, "You know I almost missed that turn, right?" She tried to explain she wasn't used to giving directions, and just as she was explaining it, we almost missed the next turn. "For real, Marcia?"

She laughed. "My bad." Then she sat up in her seat and said, "Let me pay attention, there is only one more turn anyway." We made it to her parents' house, and I understood her dad's vision. The land around their house was expansive. Like no neighbors for miles.

"I could see a little cottage for you right by that tree." I pointed after I opened her door. She elbowed me in the side. "Lay out and watch the stars at night." I looked up as we walked up the steps to the front door.

We didn't wait for anyone to open the door. Marcia used a key and let us in. "Hello," she said as we walked through the foyer.

"Joseph?" I heard a woman's voice before I saw her mother step into sight.

"Mrs. Mercy," I replied after looking down at Marcia. "Good to see you again."

"You too, dear," she said, giving me a gentle hug. "I didn't realize you were coming." She looked at Marcia then back to me. "But I'm glad you are here." She started walking down the hall, and both of us followed behind her. "Your sisters are in the kitchen." She looked back to me and said, "Mr. Mercy is on the back patio, maybe you can join him?" I nodded my head.

Marcia took a turn down a hallway, and her mother continued straight ahead. I followed Marcia and asked, "So, by not knowing what to tell your mother, you meant you didn't tell her anything at all?" I whispered to the back of her head.

She turned to me just as her hand reached for the doorknob of the patio, and she said, "Right." Then gritted her teeth. "Daddy," she announced as we stepped onto a patio that was more like an outdoor living area—fully decorated seats, with a brick fireplace, and a dining table set with plates, glassware, and silverware.

"Marcia." Her dad turned around with a glass in his hand and opened his arms. "Good to see you, baby." He looked to me then back to her and asked, "And you brought company?"

Marcia stepped out of his arms then stood beside me, and said, "Yes, Daddy, this is Joseph." I reached out for his hand, and she continued, "I'm going to go help get the food ready to bring out here." She looked at me and smiled softly before she left her dad and me alone.

Mr. Mercy looked to his glass and offered, "Do you drink bourbon?" I nodded my head. "Would you like a glass?" I nodded my head again. "Great, let me grab you one." He sat down on the seat and motioned for me to sit across from him. He pulled out a decanter and another glass and poured. If living life to the fullest was a person, Mr. Mercy was him.

I looked out for miles of what I expected was all of their land. Beautifully landscaped yard, framed by large trees and flowers. "This yard is amazing." I looked to my other side and added, "How far out does your land go?"

He chuckled and said, "As far as the eye can see." He shifted in his seat, and I took a sip of my bourbon as I anticipated the questions that would follow. "Tell me, how'd you meet my daughter?"

I leaned forward and said, "Actually, your wife and my mother planned for me to be her date for her birthday party." His eyes narrowed and he took a sip of his drink. "But that didn't work out."

"I bet it didn't," he scoffed. "My wife can't seem to mind her own business." He raised his glass. "But somehow, it worked out for you two, huh?"

I nodded my head, not knowing exactly what we were doing anymore, but replied, "I guess so."

"And what do you do for a living?" I figured that question would be in the lineup, and although I knew it would come, I still didn't exactly have a quick answer.

"I'm a plumber." Mr. Mercy's head cocked, but he didn't respond. "Actually, I moved home after my father passed away, and now I run the plumbing business he's had for years." I corrected, "My whole life actually."

"Walter Long?" I nodded my head at the sound of my father's

name. "Ah." He threw his hand in the air. "You are good people then." He laughed. "Me and your father went to school together."

It was my turn to cock my head. As much as my father admired *The Ferg*, he never once mentioned he went to school with him. Maybe if I had done the math I would have figured it out. "You two went to school together?" I asked to clarify.

He nodded his head. "Sure did." Then he shrugged. "Not that we were good friends or anything, but we had a couple of classes together. Chatted over work, women, a few times in the back of the class." He paused. "Wait, your mother—" He wagged his finger in the air. "Jennifer?"

"Yeah, how'd you know?" He told me how much my father talked about her during their chats, about how he was going to make her his wife, *one day*. "But doesn't every kid say something like that in high school?"

He shook his head. "No, not the way Walter said it." We both laughed. He told me a few more stories about my dad, and the few interactions they had together, before the patio door opened and out walked Marcia's sisters—food in hand.

"Alright, gentlemen, time to eat." They started placing food around the table, and Mr. Mercy stood from where we were seated and directed me to the table before he instructed, "Follow me and we can wash our hands."

We passed Marcia and Mrs. Mercy on our way inside. "Just over there, to your left, is the restroom. I'll grab the other one upstairs."

I went to the restroom and washed my hands, and then on my way back outside, I heard talking coming from what I assumed was the kitchen. As I approached, I heard a voice say, "And how did you end up bringing Joseph and not Boris?" I was too close to turn around, but made sure I walked loudly so that they'd hear me coming.

As I expected, they were silent when I entered the kitchen.

"You need help carrying anything else outside?" I looked between Marcia and her sister, Olivia, the one I met in the grocery store.

"Yeah, can you grab that tray?" Olivia pointed to a tray then looked to her sister before she disappeared.

CHAPTER FIFTEEN

MARCIA

I could have killed my sister dead for bringing up Boris's name. But Joseph didn't say anything—not a single word—about hearing her mention Boris's name. I was thinking he was too far away when she said it.

That's until we were driving home, and the small talk about my family ended. We were still miles away from my place when Joseph cleared his throat and asked, "So, who is Boris?"

In my head, I had prepared an entire speech—we are just dating; we never said we'd be exclusive; you stood me up; it isn't that serious with him or with you. But the words that fell out of my mouth sounded more like, "You heard her?"

"Unfortunately," he said softly. He sounded more wounded than I expected. And I didn't know what I expected. For him to be happy that I had another guy?

"I apologize that you overheard Liv." I paused because of all the things I knew were true, I didn't want to hurt Joseph. "Boris is a guy I met recently."

"How recently?" He turned to me briefly before looking back at the road.

"Last weekend." There was silence. I didn't elaborate and tell him the obvious—that I met Boris when I should have been on a date with him. He didn't ask for more details, likely knowing too much already.

"And you are..." His hands tapped the steering wheel again. "Dating?"

By then, he was pulling into the parking garage of my building, and as much as I had anticipated him staying and catching up with him without my family around, I was feeling all types of awkward. He parked his car then he laughed, and I just stared at him. "Brother caught me slippin'." I shrugged because that was the truth. "That's alright, he won't catch me again."

I scoffed, "Is that right?" He nodded his head. "You sound pretty confident." I didn't know what it was about him being all barbarian—me Tarzan you Jane—but I was turned all the way on, shifting in my seat to stop the throbbing between my thighs, turned on.

"Besides, I think your dad likes me." He looked at me with a wide grin. "So, there's that."

I raised my brow. Despite the throbbing in my pussy, I had to remind him, "You know I march to my own drum."

He nodded his head. "Oh, I know." He unbuckled his seat belt and stepped out of the car. When he opened my door, his hand reached in for mine and I took it. "Let me at least walk you to the door."

We were standing in front of my door as I dug my keys from my purse. "Thank you again for the invite." He leaned against the wall beside me. "Despite me finding out about someone trying to push up on my girl, I had a good time." He looked to me and slightly licked his lips.

That was it for me. My pussy had pushed past the awkwardness my mind was trying to retain. "Do you want to come in for a minute?"

He rubbed his hand across his chin and said, "Hell yeah, I want to come in."

He stepped through the door, and neither of us took any more steps into my place. Instead, we stood in front of the door, arms wrapped around each other, lips locked, my legs trying to climb him like a tree. "Yeah, I missed you too," he said when he pulled away slightly to tug at the buttons of my dress.

I smiled but pulled his face closer after he threw my dress to the ground. My hand rubbed across his facial hair—grown thicker since the last time I saw him. And my teeth tugged at his bottom lip. The kissing was glorious, but I wanted more of him. I didn't have to direct him though. He was already starting to walk toward my bedroom, slowly. When we got there he stripped, down to his bare, rock-hard ass. I sat on the bed admiring his body again, reacquainting myself with his formed muscles, and then finally, I let my eyes land on his dick, and I gasped.

"It's only been a little over a week since the last time you saw me." He reached for my chin and lifted it up. "Why are you looking like you've never seen me before?"

I rubbed my hand down the front of his stomach, stopping at each formation of an ab, before it landed in the thick of his hair. I looked up to him and explained, "My mind has been deceiving me." His eyes narrowed. "I remember all of you, but in my mind, this..." I rubbed down his shaft. "Wasn't all of *this*." And with that, I took his dick into my mouth and bobbed my head back and forth until I heard him hiss. He pulled away abruptly, and nudged me down onto the bed.

"I'm the one who is supposed to be reminding you what you have right here..." He looked down at me. "With me." He lowered to the edge of the bed and slid my panties down my legs. If territory marking was a thing you could do with your tongue and a pussy, he was doing it. And doing it well.

He ate my pussy with passion, licking between the lips and

sucking on my clit as my body reacted—that feeling of bliss and torture combined had me easing and tensing my legs around his head.

His grip around my thighs tightened, and he stretched my legs open wider. I didn't think the pleasure could increase, but as his tongue dug deeper, I squirmed under his constraint. He paused, and I heard him say, "Do you want me to stop?"

I responded, "Not at a—" And before I could finish responding, he was going back in. I thanked him accordingly. "Oh my goodness, shit." One of his hands left my thigh and traveled up my body—it landed on my chest. He took a nipple between his fingers, and I didn't have time to respond to that feeling before I felt his teeth on my clit, and I screamed his name, "Jo..."

The rest of his name was stuck in my throat as I tried to recover. "Hmm," he whispered as he made his way onto the bed. My eyes were closed, but I could feel him tucked into my side, one of his fingers tracing a trail between my chest down to my navel, and back up again.

Then he was gone, his solid imprint and the warmth of his body were missing. "Where are you going?" I whispered, my eyes still closed tightly.

He didn't respond. Instead, I heard the condom wrapper rip open. His knee nudged between my legs, opening me wide again. He hovered over me, his mouth on my neck, suckling there as I leaned my head to the side giving him more access.

His body lowered down on top of mine, and I felt his dick at the edge of my pussy, then gently inside, slowly, deeper. Until I felt him all the way inside, and I sucked in my breath. My hands went to his chest, feeling my way around before I cupped his face and brought it down to mine to find his lips.

As he maneuvered his dick in and out, my tongue navigated his mouth. We were in a groove before he abruptly stopped kissing me, pulled out, and wrapped his arm around my waist. He flipped me over onto my belly before I had a chance to grasp what was happening. I couldn't hear what he was muttering from behind me, but I felt everything he had to say when he was deep inside of me again.

My ass was slapping back into him as I balanced myself on my forearms, my head lying on my pillow. I was thankful for the pillow as he slowly pulled out, and without warning, slammed back into me, causing the tingling that was building up to release. Although I wanted to collapse onto the bed, I continued balancing myself.

Joseph's hands gripped my waist tighter, and I felt him closer before I heard him grumble and pause. He lay beside me and his heavy arm draped across my belly. "Naw," he mumbled, "you won't catch me slippin' again."

I laughed and rubbed my hand across his arm. Joseph was the easygoing, caring, humble spirit. Lying beside him, I didn't even consider Boris in the equation. "Alright," I whispered into the air, but knew he likely didn't hear me because my whisper was met with a soft snore. I joined him in a slumber of my own.

I woke up and panicked, thinking I had to be somewhere or do something. I opened my eyes and looked around the room. "What?" I narrowed my eyes at the clock beside my bed. *Ten o'clock.* I looked to my window, shades still open, and the street-lights shining through. Then I heard water running in my bathroom and remembered that I fell asleep with Joseph beside me. I looked down to my still naked body, and pulled a sheet up to my neck.

Joseph walked out of the bathroom fully dressed and smiled at me as he stood in the doorway. "I should get out of here." I nodded my head. "Can I come by tomorrow," he added, "after work?"

I tried to think of my schedule and what I had planned, but the fog from my nap was still taking over. Assuming I was free, I said, "Sure." He walked over to my bedside, leaned down, and pecked my lips. I reached up and rubbed the side of his face, letting my eyes gently close. "See you tomorrow."

I spent most of the day thinking about Joseph, and what our next interaction would be, but as I sat at my desk an alert came to my phone.

Boris: Pick you up at 7?

I scrolled up in my text with him and realized I had agreed to go on a date with him—on a Monday. I gritted my teeth and contemplated who I wanted to spend my time with, and as I was trying to think of a way to let the other one know something came up, my office door opened.

"Oh." Nic stood in front of my desk. "Why do you have that look on your face?" She scrunched her nose, likely mimicking the look I had on my face. "Looking like you just found out your favorite show was cancelled." Then she paused and said, "Wait, they aren't cancelling *Love in the City*, are they?" I shook my head and shrugged my shoulders. "I forgot you don't watch it."

"What?" I finally mouthed. "Never mind all that, what did you come in here for?"

She looked up into the air and then announced, "Right, the new marketing campaign." Her smile widened. "We'll need to close headquarters for a day."

She could have announced that in our staff meeting, but instead, she was bringing it to me at the end of the day like it was a simple request. "A day? Close?" I looked at my door then back to her. "Are you crazy?"

She threw her hands in the air defensively. "Hear me out."

Nic was good at her job, most of her marketing efforts yielded results beyond our expectations. Although closing HQ would give Mama Mercy a heart attack, I trusted Nic knew what she was doing. "Okay," I responded. "If you think this is the best way forward for the campaign." She smiled and nodded her head.

But when she didn't turn to leave, I asked, "There's more?"

To that, she sat at the chair across from my desk, and her eyes widened. "Damn, you'd think I was bothering you." She rolled her eyes. "Sheesh."

I looked at my watch and replied, "It's almost the end of the day." Then I looked at her. "Don't you have something to do?"

"Not until you tell me why your face was all twisted up when I came in here." She started to relive the day before. "I mean, you had a fine ass man meet your parents, seemed to hit it off very well with your daddy." She smirked. "I'm sure he laid it down afterwards." She winked. "So, what's the problem?"

I cringed slightly, and her mouth dropped. "Oh, you still got ol' boy on the side, huh?" She shook her head. "What a tangled web we weave." She leaned forward and whispered, like somebody else was in the room and could hear her, "What are you going to do?"

"That's the million-dollar question." I sighed. "I kinda double booked myself today. And..." I rolled my eyes. "Somebody let it slip that Boris was a factor, and now he's on Joseph's radar."

She narrowed her eyes. "Somebody?" I told her how Joseph overheard Liv and I talking in the kitchen. "Oh." She paused. "Is that why you all came out of the house looking suspect?"

I shrugged. "Maybe."

She laughed. Placed her hand over her mouth and continued laughing at my expense. With her hand raised, she finally said, "Now I know why you are in here looking like you are about to stroke out."

"You aren't helping." I looked down at my phone. "I don't know if I should cancel on Boris or Joseph."

"Okay, what'd you have planned with Boris?" I explained that we were going out on a date, likely dinner. "Okay, basic."

"But I'm probably just kicking it at home with Joseph."

"Well then." I knew whatever she was about to suggest was not going to work because, well, because Nic. But she confirmed when she offered, "Dinner with Boris and dessert with Joseph."

"I'm not built for all that, and..." I looked down at my watch. "It's Monday, and one date alone will already be doing too much knowing that I have to be here bright and early tomorrow."

"Stop acting like an old lady." She scowled. "If you want to make this work and come out at the end with your guy, you have to treat it like *The Bachelorette*." She grinned. I told her she watched too much damn TV, and she replied, "Maybe you should watch more and you wouldn't be over here stuck."

She stood from her seat and hovered in my doorway. "Who will get that last rose?" She winked then added, "I will definitely be tuning in to this finale."

I thought about her suggestion briefly before I decided, if it would work, I had to be in control of the evening.

Marcia: How about I meet you there?

I had agreed to meet Boris at a restaurant in Rolling Hills, and as soon as our meal was over, I'd go back home and Joseph could come over. It was a well-thought-out plan. Or so I thought.

I pulled up to the restaurant and walked inside. I stood at the hostess stand and looked around, then saw Boris seated alone in the back of the restaurant. "I'm meeting with him," I told the lady standing in front of me.

As I walked away, I could have sworn I heard her say, "Lucky bitch." But I kept it moving anyway.

Boris stood and opened his arms when I reached the table. As I let his arms wrap around my waist, I inhaled his scent. The Tom Ford cologne smelled heavenly on him. "I was starting to think you were going to stand me up."

I pulled back and looked down at my watch. A few minutes past seven o'clock. "I'm right on time." I looked to him with my eyes narrowed.

"Right, but when you declined my offer to pick you up..." He pulled my seat out, and I noticed the diamond-studded cufflinks in his sleeves. "I was thinking you were about to set me up."

I shook my head. "No, I just have something to do after we wrap up here." The answer was vague but probably didn't ease his feelings.

He just nodded his head and waved the waitress over. Boris was different from Joseph—in style, mannerisms, and demeanor. I looked at him smile between asking the waiter for a vintage wine.

I looked between him and the waiter and said, "I don't think I have it in me to finish a bottle tonight."

He shrugged and said, "We don't finish it, we don't finish it," nonchalantly. The waitress smiled and walked to the bar. "What do you feel like eating tonight?" His nose crinkled. "Not that this place has too much to offer." Although I didn't have an affinity to the restaurant, I was offended. It was in Rolling Hills, and I'd been there on more occasions than I could remember. The food was decent and the people were even better.

"Don't come into town knocking our establishments," I said with my brow raised.

"You're right, I forgot this is your hometown." He laughed. "I wouldn't want to offend you."

"Exactly," I said curtly. "The scallop risotto is good." Then I listed off a few of their other specialty dishes and said, "I'd recommend any of them."

"Scallop risotto sounds like a winner." He looked around the restaurant. "I'm not sure I could ever live in a town this small." His eyes locked with someone, then he added, "Do you know everyone in here?"

I cocked my head to the side and said, "Really?" Then sighed,

"Rolling Hills is small," I bit the side of my mouth, "but not that small."

But just as I was saying how it wasn't that small, I looked over his shoulder and saw Joseph walking toward the bar. My eyes widened. "What happened?" Boris looked over his shoulder and then back to me. "You okay?"

I wanted to shrink under the table, or hide behind the menu, anything to get away from what could possibly unfold if Joseph turned his gaze around the restaurant. "Yeah," I said softly, not wanting my voice to carry to the bar.

Thankfully, the waitress returned, standing between the bar and our table, giving me a minute to think through a plan. Different scenarios were running through my head, but I dismissed them when they all ended with Joseph and Boris in a standoff in the middle of the restaurant—although neither seemed like the confrontational type.

"I think she'll have the scallop risotto," I heard Boris's voice repeat when the words wouldn't leave my mouth—they were actually somewhere caught in my throat. I nodded my head, and the waitress smiled and walked away, leaving me completely vulnerable. "You sure you're okay?"

Our eyes connected, and I confidently said, "Of course," then I lied with a little less confidence, "Just suddenly remembered something I forgot to do at work."

Boris nodded his head, and as his head bowed, my eyes landed elsewhere in the restaurant—Joseph. And his dark-brown eyes, full beard, and smooth skin. *Fuck.*

CHAPTER SIXTEEN

JOSEPH

My feet were propped up on my desk, plumber's tape twirling between my fingers, and the invoices I needed to get out were hidden behind the screensaver of my computer. I was staring out of the window looking into the parking lot where our trucks—Long's Plumbing emblazoned on the side—were parked. Never since being back in Rolling Hills had I considered my career choice—running the family business—a negative.

But there was something about the way Marcia sat across from dude, who I assumed was Boris, in the restaurant. There was something about her confidence with the dude who looked like he stepped straight out of a *GQ Magazine*. Not that I was judging the dude, but he had drip. The bottle of wine, more than I'd probably drop on some liquor, sitting casually on the table. As he sat across from my girl, or who I thought was my girl, leaned back in his seat.

Had it been any other time, or maybe if she hadn't put me off until late into the night, like I was her...*booty call*. Maybe I wouldn't be pissed.

I threw my feet off my desk and yelled out to Alonzo, "Yo,

come here." I was leaning on my desk when he walked in through the door with his chest all puffed out.

"Man, you know," he looked at me square in the eyes and reminded me, "your daddy never even used to call my name like that." His arms were across his chest. "Not even once."

I shook my head and said, "My bad," with a lowered voice.

He shrugged then said, "What'd you need anyway?"

"Man..." My head dropped into my hands. "I think I'm the side piece."

"Side piece of what?" Alonzo repeated before I heard him take a few steps closer to the desk. I looked up and his eyes widened. "Oh shit, *the side piece*," he shouted. "Bruh, what? Your girl stepping out?" Then he laughed. "Wait, she ain't even your girl." He flung his hand in the air. "Now I know why you had all that bass in your voice." He sat across from me. "That's fucked up, man. Not another..." He paused.

I already knew what he was about to say. He was referencing my ex, the one who cheated on me. "She was at the spot last night with a dude she just met, after she told me she was too busy to meet up with me earlier." As I said it out loud, I got more upset.

"How you know all that?" His face twisted to the side. Then I had to explain my run in with her at the restaurant. "Damn, that's some shit. Rolling Hills ain't that big." Then he emphasized, "I mean, in Houston, I could see."

I put my hand up to stop him from comparing my ex and that situation to Marcia. "You're right, it's not."

"So, what'd you tell her when you saw her?" I looked out the window. "She doesn't know you saw her?" I didn't turn to face him. "You didn't say shit?"

"I turned around and saw her, she saw me. I finished my drink, grabbed my food to go." I hunched my shoulders. "And I haven't talked to her."

"Damn." We both sat there for a minute. He interrupted the

silence to ask, "What are you going to do? Stop fucking with her?" When my reply didn't come quickly, he said, "Damn," then stood and walked out my office.

I grabbed my keys and left out behind him. We didn't have any more calls for the day, so instead of sticking around, I drove to the one person who probably wouldn't say what I needed to hear but would at least fill my stomach. "Mama?" I said as I entered the front door and didn't hear her in the living room like I expected. Usually, early afternoon she'd be tuned into a re-run of *Law & Order*. "Where you at?" I said a little louder when she wasn't in the kitchen either.

I heard noise coming from her bedroom as I crept down her hall. But when I heard, "Reggie," followed by a high-pitch giggle, I stopped dead in my tracks. *The fuck?* I couldn't move. My feet were frozen. Then I heard a deep voice, followed by my mama's laughter again. *Hell naw.*

"Mama," I yelled to make sure they both could hear me. I heard shuffling and mumbling before my mama finally made her way to the hallway.

"Jojo." She patted her hair. "It's the middle of the day, why aren't you at work?"

I couldn't hide the scowl on my face as I pointed to her room. I stared at her door expecting 'Reggie' to make an appearance, and when he didn't, I asked, "Is that your man?"

My mama walked toward me, with her hand on my chest, she whispered, "Let's go into the kitchen." I followed behind her, but not without looking over my shoulder first. "First, tell me why you are here in the middle of the day and not handling the business." Her eyebrow was arched. "Or is there something you needed my help with?" For as long as my father ran the business, she worked the books—on the side initially, then full time when the company became more successful. But after he passed away, she left it all to me—administration and operations. Operations weren't as difficult because we had senior level people who didn't need any direction, then there was Alonzo. "Did something happen?"

"What?" I asked. She looked at me with her head tilted to the side. "Jojo, why are you here?" Her tone sounded agitated—like I was interrupting something.

"Didn't realize I had to have a reason to come see my mama in the middle of the day." I leaned into the kitchen counter. "But you're right, I wanted to talk to you about something. It can wait though." I pointed to the hallway, surprised ol' dude hadn't tried to creep by yet. "What's going on with you and dude?"

My mom walked over to the refrigerator and opened it. She pulled out a few containers and set them on the counter in front of me. "Hungry?"

"You think you can feed me and I'm going to forget you have a dude all up in your room?" I laughed. "A dude who apparently can't face me." I opened the containers—beef stew, potatoes, cornbread. "Food does look good, though, and I will take a plate. But I need you to start talking."

She guffawed. "I need to start talking?" She stood in front of me and leaned into the counter until my eyes met hers. "Don't forget you're in my house, and I'm your mother."

I nodded my head. "You're right." I nodded again. "I apologize for being in your business." I stared at her for a moment, feeling like a chastised kid and contemplating telling her what I came for in the first place.

She smiled, slightly. "I get it. It's hard, and I thought I'd just stay alone for the rest of my days." She looked up to the ceiling and added, "But God saw fit otherwise." She moved around the counter and put her hand on my back. "Now, what had you running to my house in the middle of the day?" She pulled her head back and said, "That girl."

I took a deep breath and nodded my head. "Yeah." I decided

my mama was the one I needed to talk to, despite the fact that she was up in the house with a whole other man. "I don't know what went wrong." My mom took a seat on a barstool and nodded toward the food. I piled my plate high, warmed it, and sat beside her. "I am really feeling Marcia."

"But?"

"But, somewhere I slipped up and she has started talking to another guy."

My mama's eyes widened. "I told you if you were interested, it's not how you feel, it's how you show it." I felt ashamed but had to tell her the slip up was the night I was at her house. "Oh, over here minding my business instead of your own?" She shook her head. "I warned you that wouldn't end well."

"I mean, damn." I paused as my mama cocked her head. "Sorry. I was just going to say, if checking on you is the cause of all of this, is she even worth it though?"

She shrugged. "Eventually, when you find a wife, she should be your first priority." I didn't like the thought of that at all. "But you're right, I'd hope the woman you'd end up with wouldn't mind the fact that you are a caring son." She reached out and placed her hand over mine. "A little overbearing, but caring, and if you care for me that much, you'd likely care for her that much too."

"After my last relationship though..." Her eyebrow cocked. "I was thinking fighting for her was what I needed to do, show her I won't let her go so easy."

"But?"

"I don't know. Is that necessary? Love shouldn't be this hard."

"Love. Jojo?" She clapped her hands. "Is my baby in love?" I felt like I was a toddler taking his first shit on the potty, but I couldn't stop the smile that was spreading across my face. "Have you told her?" I shook my head, because the truth was I wasn't sure if I was in love with her.

"It's only been a couple of months."

"You know," she looked toward the hallway before she continued, "your father told me we'd be married when we first met." Her eyes gently closed and when they re-opened, they were a little misty. I wrapped an arm around her shoulders and tucked her into me. "I don't think love has to have an extended timeline to mature. It's usually your brain catching up with your heart anyway." I kissed her forehead. "But if it's meant to be"—she looked up to me— "it'll be."

"So back up then, right? Let it come to me?" I looked down into her eyes as she sat up in her seat.

"If you believe that's what you need to do, then yes." She bit the side of her mouth. "She'll realize either she wants everything you have to offer, or she won't, but no matter how hard you push up on her, she has to make that decision." She sighed. "Be willing to make that decision."

I nodded my head along as she gassed me up. "You're just saying that 'cause I'm your only son."

"Tanya could call and describe a guy, if he had any of the qualities you have, I'd hope she'd choose him."

I smiled. "Speaking of Tanya, where is she?" My little sister made it a habit to call me at least once a week, and I hadn't heard from her in over a week. "You've talked to her, right?"

My mom's eyes rolled. "Ms. Tanya has found a guy."

I gasped. "What?"

She shook her head. "He's nothing like you, dear," she warned. "In fact, he reminds me of Alonzo."

My eyes widened. "Whoa, what's wrong with Alonzo?" When her head cocked, I had to admit, "Okay, maybe he is a little rough around the edges."

Before she could go into more detail about my little sister's love interest, I heard shuffling toward the back of the house.

"Alright, dear, you got what you need?" She stood from her seat and began putting the containers back in the refrigerator.

I took one last bite of my plate before I raked the rest into the trashcan. "Yeah, Mama, I got what I need." As much as I wanted to linger and make ol' Reggie tire of her bedroom, I kissed her on the forehead and told her, "Thanks. I love you."

She stood in the doorway as I walked to my car. Over my shoulder, I said, "I hope he treats you as good as my dad did." She smiled before waving and closing the door.

CHAPTER SEVENTEEN

MARCIA

After weeks of bragging about Sur, Boris convinced me to go on a date with him there, in the *big city*. I didn't have much else to do after my Saturday boutique shopping, so I called him up and told him to send me an address in Sur to meet him at.

But as I drove through Dear Creek, and entered into Sur, it wasn't long before the cityscape was behind me and I felt like I was entering the suburbs. I passed by beautifully landscaped houses, and when I realized I was nowhere near a restaurant or public establishment, I told Siri, "Call Boris."

"Are you here?" he asked before greeting me.

"I'm not exactly sure where *here* is supposed to be, but I'm rolling through a neighborhood."

"Right." He didn't elaborate.

"You sent me the address to your house?" I asked, my voice cracking slightly.

"Yeah, one of the best places in Sur is my home." I rolled my eyes and shook my head. "But don't worry, we won't stay long. I thought you could just park your car here and we'd hop in mine."

"Okay," I finally said. "I think I'm pulling up now." I

narrowed my eyes at the numbers hung on the wooden arch of the bungalow. I parked my car in his expansive driveway and couldn't imagine why a young, single guy would want a house that large.

He opened the door before I knocked, with a wide grin on his face—and despite his cockiness, he was fine as hell. His too tight t-shirt had his chiseled chest on display. "Want a tour before we head out?" he asked, walking away from me.

"Sure," I shouted to his backside.

He stopped in the living room, and noted the large television mounted on the wall. "Unless you'd rather stay in and watch a movie?" He wriggled his brow and I shook my head. "Maybe one night," he said with a shrug. I followed behind him as he pointed out the lavish upgrades in his house. "Although I didn't build this house from scratch, the architect did an amazing job with the selections," he said as we entered a room that looked like a playroom.

"You have parties for your patients?" I asked, wondering why there was a stack of toys in his house.

He laughed then said, "No, I don't, but maybe I should." He grabbed a tiny basketball from the middle of the floor and said, "I have a set of twins."

"A set of twin what?" I looked around the room in disbelief. Not once had he mentioned kids. But the size of the house made sense considering it was occupied by a whole family.

"A boy and a girl." I looked at the kitchen set perfectly placed in the corner of the room.

I placed my hand to my forehead. "I'm trying to remember when you mentioned that before."

He shook his head. "You won't remember, because I didn't." He found a seat in a chair that was too tiny for his large stature and sat awkwardly. "Join me for a minute?" I chose to sit, a little further away from him, on the floor. "I don't usually invite women to my house." His cocky exterior was melting away—he seemed more like the guy I met at the speed-dating event, humble, sweet, casual. "Being a young dad is a lot, but having two, sometimes that can throw a woman off."

"It's more likely the baby mama." I nodded my head. "Most certainly the baby mama." I hunched my shoulders, feeling like I was channeling Nic when I added, "Nobody wants to deal with baby mama drama."

He laughed, but then he stopped and the grin on his face faltered. "I guess you are right, about the assumption of baby mama drama." He shook his head. "But that's not her, we are cool. Have a nice agreement, and little to no drama, other than her fussing at me for spoiling my kids."

"And you were married?"

He fidgeted in his seat, likely growing uncomfortable in the small chair. "Are, we are married." My eyes grew wide, and I was on my feet headed toward the door when he said, "Our divorce isn't final yet."

My feet continued walking as the thoughts swirled in my head. All of his undesirable traits were at the forefront, but that one was the straw that was breaking the camel's back. Then when I finally reached his front door, it dawned on me. I didn't have all those concerns with Joseph. It was like I was awakened from a deep sleep.

Joseph wasn't talking to me after he spotted me out with Boris, and that was understandable. But why did I continue with Boris when I knew our personalities weren't vibing? It's the reason why I kept moving toward the door when Boris said, "Hold on, don't leave."

"It's not that you have kids, and didn't mention them, but that you have a wife. You're not completely divorced." I shook my head and continued, "And didn't think I'd want to know that." I took a deep breath. "That I deserved to know that?"

Simply, he said, "Fair." He took a few steps closer to where I was, my hand on his front door. "I'm trying to move on from that."

"Until you do..." I shrugged. "There's nothing I can do for you." I opened the door and walked out.

On my drive back home, I called the girls. Nic first. "Get Liv on the phone."

"Hello to you too, ma'am," she said with a scoff. "Acting more and more like your mama every day." Before I could properly greet her, she had already went to connect Liv to the call. "Can you meet me at my house?" I looked at the navigation then said, "In thirty minutes."

Liv tried to negotiate timing with me because she had somewhere to be, but Nic flat out told me, "Like I don't have something to do on a Saturday night. I mean, it's bad enough that I see you two heffas Monday through Friday, and most Sundays," she continued grumbling.

"Fine. Don't come." I turned my attention to Liv. "Can you be there?"

Nic yelled, "It's like that?" She gasped. "This must be serious. I'll be there in thirty."

I made it to my house in less than thirty minutes and went straight to the kitchen to grab a bottle of wine. First, I poured myself a hefty glass, gulped it, and then pulled out two more glasses for the girls.

"Whatever this is, if you make it quick I can still make my plans in an hour," Liv said as she barreled through my door. I handed her a glass of wine and she paused, looking at me with her head cocked. "This is either really fucking bad or really fucking good." She took a sip of her wine and said, "Oh, the good shit. Damn." She sat her purse on the kitchen counter. "What happened?"

"Nic should be here soon." I took a deep breath, and a long

sip of my wine. "Where are you headed in an hour?" I asked, hoping to give Nic a few minutes to arrive.

"Oh, this random art exhibit is opening on Main Street." I envied my youngest sister. She stayed very active in the city. She knew about any and everything going on. "I know a couple of the artists," she said with a grin.

"Maybe I'll go check it out next weekend." Then I heard a knock at the door. "Finally," I whispered as I pulled the door open.

"Good." She came through the door with her eyes on my glass of wine. "I'm glad there's wine." She walked into the kitchen and grabbed the empty glass on the counter and immediately filled it. "Now, what's going on that required me to come over here when I could have been on my couch scrolling through Chris's Instagram feed?"

Before I got started, I asked, "What?" Chris was her on again, off again, boyfriend of forever. But she mostly gave him a hard time, not wanting any of his attention. So, I asked, "Why are you scrolling his IG?" She rolled her eyes and shook her head. "Okay, fill us in on that later."

"Yes, later, I now have forty minutes before I need to leave." Liv looked between the two of us, rubbed her hand through her short hair, then said, "Spill it already, Cia."

They already had the background on Joseph and me, so there was no need to tell them nothing had changed there. "I drove to Sur today to meet up with Boris." Nic took a loud, obnoxious sip of her wine. I cut my eyes at her before I continued, "I thought we were going to meet at a restaurant or bar, somewhere public."

"Naw, that man said it's been weeks, he wants them panties." Nic laughed and Liv nodded her head.

"Whatever. I pulled up to his house and he claimed he just wanted us to drive together." I paused for a sip of wine. "He insisted on a tour."

"Of course, he did, had to get you into the bedroom some-how," Nic joked again.

I ignored her and continued, "It's a beautiful home, huge, elaborate, decorated beautifully. But like a family home. Not one I'd see as a bachelor pad for a single man his age."

"He's accomplished. Has a little money." Liv shrugged. "It makes sense."

She thought, until I said, "Then we ended up in a playroom."

"Playroom?" Nic perked up. "Like in *Fifty Shades*?" She whistled. "This man took you to the dungeon?"

I just looked at her with my eyes narrowed then blurted, "A playroom, a kids area with toys, for children."

They both had my initial response. "So he brings his patients to his house?" Liv asked.

"Same question I had." I cocked my head.

"Oh hell. That man gotta family?" Liv yelled. "Hell naw."

I nodded my head. "Twins. A boy and a girl."

Liv tried to make it okay by saying, "I mean, you want kids. You just won't have to pop them out."

"Hmm," Nic grunted.

"Exactly. But that's not even all of it." I took a longer sip of my wine. "He's married."

"What?" they both yelled in unison.

I didn't let them dwell there long. I clarified with, "Getting a divorce, but right now, married."

"And after you found all that out, what'd you do?" Liv asked with her hand on her chin as she leaned on the counter.

"Told him that was an absolute no go." I shrugged. "And I left. Walked up out of there."

Nic had a serious look on her face when she said, "You mean this man managed to have an entire family, and not slip up about it, not once?" Her eye twitched. "But you go to one dinner, trying to date two guys, and get found out." She shook her head. "That's why we can't trust dudes."

"I don't know," I sighed. "He had a lot going for him, seemed like the ideal guy." I didn't have to list off all of Boris's attributes because Liv and Nic had already started to repeat them. "But..." Liv sat back in her seat and waited for me to speak, but Nic was already smacking her lips. "His cockiness."

Nic scrunched her nose. "His cocky met your cocky and that wasn't cool, huh?" I narrowed my eyes. "Oh." She looked to Liv. "She doesn't realize she's cocky too."

Liv took the last sip of her wine before reaching over the counter and placing the empty glass in my sink. "I have to go, I'll catch up with you two later." She grinned and walked to the door. Over her shoulder, she yelled, "Should have stuck it out with Joseph." Then she took it one step further before she shut the door behind her. "He's brother-in-law material."

I looked to Nic and said, "Brother-in-law material, what does that even mean?" I grabbed the bottle of wine and my glass and started to pour.

Nic scoffed and looked down at her watch like she had somewhere to be. "I guess I have time to elaborate." I laughed and shook my head. "It means that Boris seems like the logical choice. You know, successful, notable career. Nice looking Alpha man. Seems like he has it all together, on the outside. But Joseph, that man right there is hubby material. He's humble enough to put you first, but strong enough to lead when he needs to. He'd be the one we could call when some shit goes down at home and need a man's help. He'd be there." She cut her eyes at me.

"Says the person who told me to date both guys." I threw my hands up in the air. "I can't with you right now."

"And when have you ever taken my advice?" Her eyes widened. "Ever?"

I thought about it, and then shrugged. "So I shouldn't even

ask you what I should do next?" She shook her head. "Great." I sighed. "Tell me what's going on with Chris." She went on about how she thought he might have a new girlfriend. "And you know this because?"

"He stopped calling me." I couldn't hold the laughter. But Nic wasn't feeling me laughing at her expense. "Ugh." Her arms went across her chest.

"My bad, it's just you seem more confused than I do out here in these relationship streets."

She sighed. "It's something about the thrill of the chase for me though." She rolled her neck. "Him calling, me not answering, us running into each other in public and rushing to his house to fuck afterward."

I threw my hand up. "Wait, what?" She laughed. "I don't even want to know." She described how dick deprived she had been in the last couple of weeks.

"My thirtieth birthday is coming up, though, so maybe I'll just wait for Mama to deliver my man." We both looked at each other and sighed.

Then I had to remind her, "You know you haven't even turned twenty-nine yet, right?"

"I know." She nodded her head. "It'll be here before you know it." Then her nose crinkled. "Have you ever thought about our age difference? I think about how Mama was popping us out with the quickness." Then she smiled. "At thirty."

"Guess that explains things a bit." I shrugged. "Guess I would have been close to having some kids with Boris." I laughed. "A whole bonus mommy?" I slumped forward onto the counter. "I can't believe he has kids, and a wife."

Nic and I joked around about Boris, until she yawned and said, "I should get home." She looked down into her empty wine glass, one that had been emptied three times, at least. "This vintage shit is strong." She laughed as she stood from her seat.

"Sure you can drive home?" She rolled her eyes and I threw my hands up.

Before she walked to the door, she said, "Just call him." My eyes narrowed. "We just said not to listen to my advice, but I think it's simple enough. Call Joseph."

CHAPTER EIGHTEEN

JOSEPH

I looked at my phone vibrating across the kitchen counter, and I saw her name. I didn't jump to pick up the phone like I expected I would if she ever called. I thought I'd be more excited to talk to her but by the time I picked up the phone, all I was able to give her was a simple, "What's up?"

She was either disappointed or surprised I answered, because she stuttered when she replied, "Hey, hey Joseph."

"Hey, Marcia." There was a long pause before either of us said anything else, and because she was the one who called, I waited.

"I thought this would be easier." I didn't expect those words, or the ones that followed. "I need to apologize." I could hear her shuffling around in the background. "I didn't handle any of this the right way." I allowed her to continue, and the words fell from her mouth. "I shouldn't have been so caught up in the fact that you couldn't make our dates. And I shouldn't have tried to date both you and..." She stopped before saying dude's name, and a part of me was thankful. I didn't need a name to go along with the face that had been popping up in my mind since the night I saw him sitting across from my...from her. "Anyway, you've been heavy on my mind, and I was wondering if..." But then she stopped, and it was silent. I couldn't even hear her shuffling around anymore.

"Marcia?" I said, thinking the phone disconnected.

"I'm still here. I don't know, this doesn't feel right either."

"What does it feel like?" I wanted to know, because I know for me, at least, I wasn't feeling what I was thinking I'd feel. Something was missing.

"Feels like we need a reset. Start from scratch. Clear expectations and communication." She kinda chuckled. "Like I need to just bump into you again."

"You mean you need me to knock on your door again?"

She laughed and quickly said, "Not that part."

Hearing her laugh lifted something off my shoulders. I wasn't feeling as tense anymore. "What do you suggest?" I asked after taking a seat on my couch.

"This will sound bizarre, but how about we leave it up to fate?"

And because I had no idea what she was referring to, the game plan sounded shoddy. "And what exactly do we do until then?"

"We go with the flow." It was completely unlike Marcia—the planner. She had a plan for her plans, typically. After all, she managed the operations of her family business and that shit ran like a well-oiled machine, at least that's how she described it.

"I don't know." I leaned forward on the couch. "Bumping into you at the restaurant didn't work out in my favor," I teased. Then, before she could respond, I had to know what happened to buddy. "What happened to you and dude anyway?"

"It wasn't right." Then I considered how she was on the phone with me hoping fate reunited us.

"And we are?" I asked honestly.

"Something is telling me we'll soon find out." I was intrigued, or ready to fuck, either way I was up for the fate plan.

"Okay, guess I'll see you around," I said before hanging up the phone.

The rest of that night and throughout the week, I thought about the different places we'd been together, or places I knew she frequented. Like the boutique, happy hour at the restaurant where I saw her and dude, and the yoga studio. But I didn't want to fake fate, I didn't want to make us bump into each other. I wasn't quite persuaded we needed to be randomly reunited either. I would have been okay with us picking up where we left off—then a wild night of make-up sex to get us back on track.

As I described the grand idea to Alonzo, I was even less convinced of the plan. He sat beside me as we rode to one of the jobs on the outskirts of the city. "Still haven't bumped into ol' girl yet?" I shook my head. "Hmm...and in the meantime you aren't talking to her on the phone either?" I shook my head again, a little harder. "That's a bullshit plan if you ask me."

Then I reminded him, "And I didn't ask you." I pulled into the driveway of the dated bungalow and thought about all the work we'd be doing on the plumbing of the house. "This project will likely have me too busy to think about the situation anyway."

Alonzo called me on my bullshit. "Man, too busy to think about fucking?" He opened the door and said, "Not that much work in the world." He laughed as he made his way up the sidewalk to the front door. He knocked, and started speaking to the woman who answered the door as if he wasn't just talking shit on his walk up the sidewalk. "Yes ma'am, Long Plumbing." She nodded her head then looked over his head to where I stood carrying a toolbox.

Her eyes met mine and she said, "Thank God, these pipes need work." The smile on her face that followed didn't seem like she was in distress. Alonzo turned to me and cocked his head. If it was a plumbing innuendo, we'd heard it, at least a few times before. Thanks to the name of our business, *Long Plumbing,* they were probably even worse. But some, when said, had a little more emphasis. "Come on in." Despite her emphasis, I remained professional.

Alonzo, though, he made sure I heard what I heard. "You may not have to wait on ol' girl to show up, looks like fate is twisting in your favor after all." He laughed as I walked ahead of him, following behind Ms. Denton.

"I noticed this spot on the ceiling"—she pointed above our heads in the hallway—"a few days ago." The spot was fairly large, and likely took longer than a few days to accumulate.

"And on the second floor above here?" Alonzo asked, our standard question before trucking through a client's house.

"The laundry room." She frowned. "Could it be a problem with my washing machine?" she asked, as if it was her first time considering it.

Alonzo nodded his head, but I responded, "It could be the washing machine itself or the plumbing to the washing machine. This spot, though"—I pointed above my head—"seems like it's been accumulating for a while."

"I just returned home after a month on the road." She looked between the two of us. "I travel for work."

That made more sense, and I nodded my head. "We'll take a look and let you know if we can resolve the issue with the plumbing." But then I had to drop the information nobody wanted to hear. "But the damage to this area in your ceiling will need someone else." I looked to Alonzo then back to her. "We have some contacts you can call." She sighed but nodded her head. "Take us upstairs?"

Her grin had returned as she said, "I'd be happy to."

Alonzo cleared his throat as he followed behind the two of us up the stairs and to the laundry room. We moved around the washing machine to get to the connection. Alonzo would usually be talking trash about not being the muscle, but Ms. Denton decided to stick around and watch us. "We can come grab you when we've finished looking it over." I looked toward her then added, "If you want." I added in a slight shoulder shrug in hopes she'd take me up on the offer to give us space to work.

She smiled and announced, "Yeah," then she looked down the hallway before saying, "I'll just be in my bedroom." Alonzo's head snapped around before she could even leave the entry of the laundry room, and when he looked back to me, his eyes were the size of saucers.

"Damn, man." He shook his head. "I don't think she could be sending a clearer message."

Ms. Denton was sexy as fuck—beautiful caramel-brown skin, a bright smile, and her body was hitting in all the right places. But I was there to finish a job. "Man, listen," I said to Alonzo, "that's not it." Then I pointed to the bend in the connection. "That's it right there." Not exactly a problem for Long's Plumbing, but where there was suspicious water, we got the call. "You can let her know she needs a new hose."

"I can let her know?" Alonzo stood with his arms across his chest. "Pretty sure it's you she'd rather hear it from." He tapped the top of the washing machine. "What is it?" He stopped tapping then pointed. "We aim to please?" He was quoting one of our value principles.

"She'll be happy when you tell her we aren't charging her for the visit."

"Not charging her for the visit?" Alonzo repeated and cocked his head. "Man, look, I hope you bump into your lover girl soon, because she has you out here talking greasy."

I laughed and walked out of the laundry room with him closely behind me. Before he could follow me down the stairs, I nodded toward the bedroom and warned, "Stay in the hallway," in a low whisper.

His eyes said it all, but he said, "Just trying to aim to please."

I stopped walking down the stairs and said, "But this isn't McDonald's, she can't have it her way." He laughed, and I continued down the stairs with the same hope—that I'd bump into Marcia soon.

CHAPTER NINETEEN

MARCIA

What the hell was I thinking? Fate? Destiny? A third time's the charm happily ever after? I rolled my eyes as I looked in the mirror and reapplied my lipstick—just in case that chance encounter would happen.

But why would it? It'd been weeks and Joseph was nowhere in sight. I had started to think maybe he left town. Then Nic reminded me, "No, you just think we are from a town in the country somewhere with a fifty-person population." I remembered that as I adjusted my shirt, making sure my chest was on proper display. Then, I sighed. I had his phone number, I could just call him and end my misery.

I grabbed the dresses I planned to purchase, and walked out of the dressing room determined to contact Joseph. In my haste, I didn't even notice anyone in my path to the register. "Excuse me," I heard an older woman say with a stern voice.

I looked up from my purse, making eye contact with the beautiful black woman, and whispered, "Sorry." But before I could continue on, I stared at her—her features oddly familiar.

Her smile widened the longer I stared, and I apologized. "You look like someone I know," I finally offered.

She shrugged her shoulders and said, "I don't get that often." Then she joked, "I hope she's just as wise, but half as beautiful." I scrunched my nose, and she clarified, "You know, I don't need the competition." I laughed as I continued to the register. Then I heard her say, "How about this one, Jojo?"

It wasn't the name that caught my attention, but the voice of the man who responded that had me turning around, a full one-eighty, to see him walk toward her from across the boutique.

He had a blank stare on his face, as if he was bored with the activity. But when she raised the dress, his mouth grew into a wide grin—just like hers had earlier. I looked between the two of them and realized the resemblance was undeniable.

"Joseph?" I said softly. Both of them turned toward me.

She looked to him, and he looked to me, his eyes blinking, but his feet not moving. So I walked to him. "You know her?" I heard the woman, presumably his mother, ask.

He looked down to her and nodded his head. "Marcia," he said, adding "Mercy" confidently behind it.

"Oh." She looked to me as I stood in front of him. "Imagine that. The two of you running into each other here, of all places." I smiled because it was the last place in the city I would have thought we would reunite.

"Hey," he greeted me, and his arms opened wide. I didn't hesitate to walk into them. "Took a little time, but we are here," he said into my ear. I heard his mom mumble something before walking away, leaving the two of us in an embrace in the middle of my favorite boutique.

I knew I heard a few, "oohs," and "ahhs," and maybe even a handclap or two from my favorite girls who worked in the shop and helped me on the weekly. I laughed and looked up to him. "Finally," was all I could manage to say. My heart felt like it was in the pit of my stomach, among the butterflies flapping rapidly.

"I'm somewhere between overjoyed and frustrated." I cocked my head at him as he explained, "My mom has been trying to get me to come with her dress shopping for a couple of weeks now." He looked back to her. "Maybe this little reunion could have happened sooner." His smile grew wide, and his tongue went across his bottom lip.

The butterflies in my stomach had nothing on the pulsing going on further south. That girl, she was ready. "Mama?" He nodded his head. "You look just like her," I said as I tried to calm all my bodily responses, as I looked across the store to where she was picking through a set of dresses.

"Where is she headed?" I asked without looking back to him.

"The Mercy Foundation Ball."

I looked up to him, and my mouth parted slightly. "Is that right?" He nodded his head. It was a few weeks until the ball, and even I hadn't started looking for a dress. It hadn't slipped my mind, but definitely wasn't on the top of it either. "Are you going along as her date?" I asked, hoping I'd have the chance to see him sporting a tuxedo.

He frowned. "That was the plan, but she recently decided she wanted to take her dude." My eyebrow hitched.

I saved my jokes because I could tell he was feeling some sort of way just by the look on his face. I placed my hand on his chest and asked, "Now that we are here, guess we have to figure out what's next."

And before I could ask, he interrupted, "Marcia." My hand felt his heartbeat against my palm—quickening. "The only thing I want to do right now is fuck you senseless." He winked, then he said, "Then I want you to know," he wagged his hand through the empty space between us, "this is it."

I narrowed my eyes. "This is it?" I repeated.

"You and me." He shook his head. "No games, no random dudes."

I emphasized, "Or ladies."

"That was never a problem before," he said matter-of-factly, and I had to look down at my feet to be sure my panties hadn't dropped to the ground. He lowered his head down to my ear and said, "Except her." He looked back to where his mother was, still shifting through dresses. "She'll always be a top priority."

"As she should be," I said.

He nodded his head. "Do you have plans tonight?"

I shook my head. "I've been leaving my evenings open." I looked away then back to him. "Just in case." He didn't respond; instead, he pulled me into his arms and my eyes instinctively closed. I inhaled his scent—his cologne, noticeable but not over-whelming, lured me in.

"Now you do." He smiled then said, "How about we cook dinner?" And by we, I assumed he meant me and him, and half of that equation couldn't cook. My eyes widened. "What?"

"Did you forget I can't really cook?" He shook his head. "So, by cook, do you mean order take-out?" Because I was good at that. I could put in an order with the quickness, make all the right menu selections, and my timing was impeccable. I always knew just how far in advance I needed to order to be sure the food arrived when it was time to eat.

"Let's find a recipe"—he shrugged—"and make it happen." His mom called out his name, and both of us looked in her direc-tion. "Asian?" He wagged his head. "Or Italian?"

He was committed to this decision, and I didn't know why I agreed, but I did when I responded "Italian" before he kissed my cheek and went over to his mom.

Before I walked out of my favorite boutique, I asked, "Should I grab the groceries?"

With a wink, he responded, "Let me take care of that."

I had some extra pep in my step as I walked to my car. My smile was stuck on my face, and I felt butterflies in my stomach. I had planned to do more shopping, but instead hurried home to make sure my kitchen was ready for what we'd prepare together.

I had all the basics for cooking—knives, pots, pans, seasonings, wine to go along with the meal. I just never used any of it. I opened my cabinets and decided to wash the dishes, just in case they were a little dusty. That took longer than expected and when I looked up at the clock, hours had passed. I decided to hop in the shower, music blaring, as I let the water beat on my shoulders.

When I stepped out and grabbed my phone, I had a missed call from Joseph. I rolled my eyes, expecting he'd be cancelling. I tried to hide my frustration when I called him back and he answered, "You called?"

He sighed then said, "I was sitting here in the store and couldn't decide which recipe we should do." He paused then said, "We got chicken parmesan."

I had chicken parmesan before, many times, but because I didn't cook, I had no idea how hard it'd be to make at home. "What's the other option?"

"The other option is baked spaghetti." And that sounded like an easier option, and I was glad when he said, "I'm leaning toward that option, to be honest."

"Good," I replied, "I think we could pull off spaghetti."

"Baked spaghetti it is then. I should be at your place in the next hour."

That gave me just enough time to finish getting dressed. "See you then."

When I heard the knock at the door, I smoothed down my pants and tugged on my shirt. I smiled at myself in the mirror as I checked my makeup, then went to the door. The look on his face when I opened the door was everything. In the store, I had to maintain my composure because his mom was nearby, but with him in my face and in my space—it was a different situation. "Come in," I said after we stared at each other for a beat. His hands were full of bags and I reached for one, but he shook his head.

"I got this," he said with confidence and his chest poked out. I closed the door after he walked past me, and I took the opportunity to take in the view from the back. Joseph wasn't one to dress in designer clothes, and likely didn't keep up with trends, but his simple look worked for him. Hell, the way his jeans fit his ass, had me thinking he should model professionally. "Alright," he said, looking over his shoulder. He laughed. "Were you just staring at my ass?" My nose scrunched and I shrugged my shoulders. "If we are going to make it through this dish, I'll have to save my comments for later." I grinned because I had already lost my appetite. Baked spaghetti sounded like a great idea, but sexing him sounded even better.

"If you insist." I picked up my phone and said, "There's still time, I could call in an order, and we could *catch up* while we wait on it."

He pulled my phone out of my grip and tugged on me until I was flush against his chest. Looking down into my eyes, he reminded me, "Don't worry, I have nowhere to be tonight." He kissed the side of my mouth. "Or in the morning." His tongue parted my lips and we were in a deep, passionate kiss, when I felt his hands grip my ass. He pulled away abruptly then said, "But first, we are going to cook this food." He laughed.

I took a deep breath and averted my eyes from his gaze. "If you insist." I went to the bags and began pulling out ingredients. "So, where's the recipe?"

He started digging in his back pocket, and I expected he would pull out his phone but when he handed me a recipe card, I looked between him and the card—scribbled with ink, slightly faded. "Mama Long's famous baked spaghetti," he announced as I looked over the card.

I looked at the recipe card then at the fresh tomato in my hand. "Wait, we are making sauce from scratch?" He nodded his head proudly. "Okay." I pulled out the remaining ingredients then said, "Did you harass your mama for this recipe?"

He turned from the stove where he had already started boiling water. "Not at all." Then he paused. "She said she was always saving them for her daughter-in-law."

I gasped, and that turned into an abrasive cough. "Daughter-in-law?" I repeated after he patted my back a few times.

He laughed. "I guess my mama is a lot like yours in that area, rushing me down the aisle."

"Oh." I felt oddly disappointed. "You aren't worried about marriage?"

He turned to the pot on the stove and dumped in the noodles. "Not yet." Granted I wasn't ready for marriage, yet, but the thought of it sounded more like a possibility with him standing in my kitchen whipping up a meal from scratch.

"Right, not yet," I mumbled under my breath, more to myself than to him.

CHAPTER TWENTY

Joseph

Maybe I shouldn't have told Marcia what my mama said, but I didn't want to lie. She did say she was saving all her best recipes for her daughter-in-law, talking about she wanted me to be able to have some of her best cooking if she wasn't around.

When Marcia damn near choked when I said it, I wanted to make sure she wasn't feeling the pressure. I tried to change the subject, laugh about our encounter earlier in the day. "Since my mama nixed me as her date to the gala, I was wondering..." I looked away from the pot of sauce I was stirring, to the counter where she was struggling with chopping the lettuce for the salad. "Wait." I stopped my trail of words. "Have you never chopped lettuce before?"

One hand was holding the knife, but the other was maneuvering the head of lettuce around the cutting board, awkwardly. She looked up to me with her eyes wide and admitted, "I should have learned how to cook." She sighed. "It looks so easy on those cooking shows though." I laughed.

"Yeah, maybe we can spend more time in the kitchen and less time at restaurants." The thought of having kids eat take-out every day flashed into my mind, and I had to ask, "Growing up, you and your sisters ate home-cooked meals, right?"

She scoffed. "You've been to my house." She reminded me of the spread her mama made. "My mom is a superwoman, hell, she does it all."

I smiled then asked, "Did you just avoid the kitchen?" She gritted her teeth.

"I mean, looking back on it now, it was a very bad decision on my part. And surprisingly, my mama didn't force us to be in the kitchen with her." She looked down to the cutting board. "But now I'm sitting here and can't even cut the lettuce."

"We'll work on those knife skills another day, but for now, you can just pull it apart and rip it up." She winced, and I knew she was thinking about how it'd look. "It's just us. When we have friends over one day, we'll get the pre-cut lettuce," I joked.

"Friends over one day?" I narrowed my eyes at her. "That actually sounds like a great idea. We should invite your home-boys over, and my sisters." She started gushing about how neat it would be if we could make a match between my friends and her sisters.

"Whoa." I raised my hand. "Maybe you should meet my friends first." I laughed, thinking about how wild Alonzo was. "Don't want your sisters pissed at me."

She nodded her head. "Good point." Then she asked, "Are we there now? The meeting friends stage?" Considering I had dinner with her family, I thought we had passed *there*, but maybe friends come after family.

"It's been a while since I've had something new, so maybe I forgot how the journey goes, but isn't meeting the dad like the final stop?"

She looked up into the air and said, "Maybe you have a point." I walked the few steps between us and opened my arms wide, wrapping them around her.

"But, whatever we have, whatever we are doing, I don't think we have to go by the book. Can't we make up our own rules?" I looked down into her eyes and they appeared to glisten—I couldn't tell if she was getting sad or overly excited. "You okay?" I asked after a pause.

"I am, and I think that's a good idea." She smiled. "We'll create our own set of rules." She shrugged. "I'm kind of tired of following the rules anyway."

I cocked my head as she tried to wriggle out of my arms, back to her corner of the kitchen. I checked on the spaghetti sauce and announced, "I think it's ready now."

She nodded her head, but that last comment she made had me curious. "Do you think you've played it too carefully up until now?"

She explained that everything she had done to date was at the direction of her mom. "I mean, you're here." She pointed to me. "Not that I mind that at all, but it's just like, when I do make moves, they are all at the direction of my mom." As she continued on about moving home and working for the family business, I poured the sauce over the noodles.

And when it felt like she was wrapping up, I asked, "What's one thing you want to do, but know your mama would have a fit about?"

Her eyes widened, and she responded, "Quit my job." I didn't expect that at all, but I should have known her job wasn't lighting her fire. I could relate, slightly. The only reason I was home was because I didn't want our family business to fail. But I always had an end date in mind, so maybe that sustained me. I shifted on my feet, then grabbed the dish and stuck it in the oven before I suggested, "Quit."

She looked at me and shook her head. After a long sigh, she admitted, "I can't." I grabbed her hand and walked us over to her couch.

"I know your mom wouldn't be happy about it, but what other reasons do you have to keep working there?" As she hesitated, I reminded her, "I know your mom would rather you be happy." She smirked. "Maybe I read her wrong, but it seems that's all she wants for each of you."

I interlaced my fingers with hers and she leaned her head on my shoulder. "Generally, yes."

I sensed we wouldn't get far with that, so instead I asked, "Okay, give me something else. Something not as life changing for you. But something you've always wanted to do but would make your mom shit a brick."

She laughed. The fingers of her opposite hand were tracing circles on my forearm. I tried to ignore it. The delicate touch had my dick growing in my pants, and I hoped she wouldn't notice.

"I don't even know," she groaned—and I knew she didn't intend to, but it sounded like a labored moan, and I had to place my arm over my pants to distract from the teepee that had hitched in my crotch. "How lame is that?" she asked, looking me straight in the eyes.

I agreed that it was pretty lame, but I didn't confirm that. Instead, I leaned into her lips and opened her mouth with my tongue. Unlike earlier in the day when we were trying to keep it PG-13 for my mama, she took it X-Rated, when she crawled into my lap and her hands went to the back of my head.

Marcia had been passionate before, but there was something a little more desperate about her kiss—something needy, and I wanted to give her everything she needed. Her moans, mixed with her grinding against my teepee, had me ready to carry her off to bed, on an empty stomach. I wrapped my hands around her waist and stood from the couch, and that didn't even interrupt our connection—her hands continued roaming, our tongues intertwined even more, and her legs were wrapped around my waist, her hips still grinding.

As I took a few steps toward her bedroom, though, the oven chimed. She pulled away from my mouth, and said, "We should eat first."

I looked at her then back to the kitchen, before I gently put her down to the ground and mumbled, "Okay." She gently laughed and led the way to the oven, removing the pan of baked spaghetti.

She stood in front of the pan, wafting the steam into her face. "If it tastes as heavenly as it smells, I will have to thank your mama myself."

I walked up behind her, peeking over her head. "I don't think she'd mind that at all."

"Consider it done." She cleared her throat then said, "I hope she isn't disappointed when I tell her I can't cook." I leaned down and kissed her neck. I felt the tip of my dick touch her back, and I was ready to pick up where we left off and make my way to her bedroom, when she said, "She probably wouldn't be thrilled about passing recipes to a woman who can't even cook." I moved to a nearby cabinet, opening and closing it, then another, and couldn't find the plates. "Do you think she'd feel some type of way about it?"

I sighed. "Where are your plates?"

Her eyes grew wide, and she scoffed, "Are you listening to me?"

I grabbed her hand and replied, "I'm listening to you, but to be honest, I don't know how my mama will feel." I hunched my shoulders. "I can certainly ask her if you think it's necessary." I cocked my head and made sure we had eye contact before I added, "But if and when I get married, it won't be dependent upon the woman's ability to cook." I thought that was a decent response, so I smiled and tried to turn back to the cabinets, but she was unmoved. "It's a teachable skill."

"What?" Her face scrunched up.

"Cooking, just like anything else, if it really bothers you, you can learn how to cook." She pointed to the next cabinet over, and I pulled out a couple of plates.

"This is really good," she said with a soft moan after we were seated with a plate of baked spaghetti, a tossed salad, and a glass of red wine.

I looked at her after I took a sip of wine, and warned, "If you want to finish it, I suggest you do it without moaning." She looked up from her plate with her eyes wide, and I added, "I don't mind warming it up and eating it later." She grinned.

"So," she took a forkful of spaghetti and placed it at the tip of her mouth, "like," her lips wrapped around the food, and as she chewed her eyes closed, and the moans were even louder than before, "this."

My fork clanked down on her expensive white China, but I didn't let that stop me from what I was about to do next. I stood from my seat and caught it before it crashed to the floor, then I stepped to her side and grabbed her hand, tugging her out of her chair. I turned her toward me, wrapped my hands around her waist, and hoisted her up around my hips. Meanwhile, she was in a fit of laughter, trying to plead, "But the food," as I walked across the condo to her bedroom.

I slammed the door behind me for dramatic effect before I placed her down gently on her bed. My hands were on the hem of my shirt as she sat staring on the bed. "You a spectator or participant in this show?"

Her eyes widened and her head cocked. But she wasted no time pulling on her own shirt, then tugging her pants off one leg at a time. I stood before her, butt ass naked, dick looking in her direction, and heard her mumble, "Gahtdamn," under her breath. I smiled and pulled her off the bed. I had a gahtdamn for her too, but instead, I whispered it into her ear, between kisses.

Her hands roamed my chest, my back, then finally landed on

my dick and when it did, I sucked in a breath, not realizing how much I missed her touch, there. That just gave her ammunition, because her touch became more intentional—her hand wrapped tightly around me, stroking, then I felt her moisture at the tip and bit my lip to keep from losing my damn mind.

"I better grab a condom," I whispered the more she teased at her entrance.

"Yes, please," she replied, her voice sounding strained. She laid on the bed, her legs stretched open, but when I returned I didn't go back to where we left off. Instead, I bent down in front of her and ran my tongue around her crevices. All I could hear were moans and hisses, while her hands rubbed the top of my head. I felt her leg quiver beside me, and instead of letting her finish like that, I stopped abruptly and moved onto the bed.

She looked up at me and pleaded, "But wait." I shook my head and gave her what she needed, pushing inside of her slowly till her eyes closed tightly and her head fell to the side. "Okay." Her hands went to my chest, then to my back as I brought my body closer to hers.

Her hips were grinding and her nails scratching across my back, and I loved every bit of it. When I felt her pussy clench around me, my thrusts became more forceful until we both were panting. "This shit right here," I whispered in her ear as her body tensed, "will make a dude fall in love," and just like that, her back arched then collapsed onto the bed.

After a few more slow strokes, I laid beside her, my eyes tightly closed. "You can't throw words around like that," she scolded through a lazy mumble.

"Words like what?" I asked. But before she could answer, my stomach grumbled and I reminded her, "We should probably finish our food, huh?"

She laughed and pulled the sheet from under her. "Yeah, food," she said as she started making her way out of the bedroom.

I searched the floor for my boxers and followed behind her back to the kitchen. She already had our plates cleared from the table and in the microwave. "Hope your mama's recipe warms well." She leaned on a cabinet beside the microwave, wrapped in her thousand-thread-count sheet, her hair all over her head, and a hazy look in her eyes. "After I eat, I'm going straight to sleep," she joked with a yawn.

My eyes danced at the thought of being back in the bed with her. But instead of assuming I could stay, I asked, "You kicking me out?"

She cocked her head as the microwave chimed. "You fed my belly and my..." She looked down then back to me. "The last thing you have to do is leave." She smiled softly.

"Good, because a meal isn't complete without dessert." I winked, grabbing one plate from the microwave and replacing it with the other. She grabbed the warmed plate and took a bite before walking over to the table.

"What, your mama doesn't have a lemon pound cake recipe she's passing on to her daughter-in-law?"

I teased, "Oh, she does, but she can't give you everything at once." This time, she didn't choke on air in response.

We sat across from each other and she probed about the other recipes she could receive in, "a marriage to Joseph Long."

In between bites, I bragged about my mama. "Well, there is this pot pie dish she makes that soothes the soul."

"Soothes the soul," she repeated, looking at me with her eyes wide. I nodded my head. "Now you know I have to try that." Her plate was clean and her fork resting beside it when she asked, "What does she have that we could serve to a few people?"

I thought back to all the big family dinners she would have, inviting both sides of the family to our house on a random weekend. "It's been a while since she's done anything for a large group of people." I thought out loud, more to myself than to Marcia.

But she asked, "Since your father passed away?" I nodded my head. "How do you think she'd feel if we invited a few friends over to your house, and gave her the opportunity to reprise those big gatherings?"

I laid my fork on my empty plate and bit my lip. "If we gave her enough notice..." I shrugged. "Maybe she'd be okay with it."

"Perfect." She didn't say much more before she stood from the chair and added, "C'mon, I need to work on getting this pound cake recipe." She dropped the sheet and walked to her bedroom—I jumped from my seat and ran right behind her.

CHAPTER TWENTY-ONE

Marcia

The Mercy Family Foundation Gala was the event for Rolling Hills. My mother spared no expenses when it came to the event—she even convinced my father it was for a good cause, and worthy of the high ass bill he was footing. But the tenth-year gala, was on supercharge, and it started to bleed into Mercy Beauty & Wellness. Our staff meetings increased from weekly to daily, and they all revolved around updates for the gala.

"Ladies," my mom said as my sisters and I were exiting the conference room. "I haven't seen your dress selections yet." She looked at each of us, and none of us replied. "Well, do we need to take a lunch break and head into the city?"

"You know, that sounds like a great idea," Nic quickly replied. Nic was the least enthused about the gala, and formal wear, so I assumed her enthusiasm was related to getting out of the office.

"Actually," Liv spoke up, "that sounds like an amazing idea. I think we all could use a little break from planning."

My desk was stacked with paperwork I needed to complete by the end of the week, nothing gala related, but because our work had become consumed with gala planning, I hadn't had time to wrap it up. I sighed, "I should stay back." Mama Mercy's eyes connected with mine, and I gave in before she could even say anything. "Okay, fine, but remember to tell my boss not to hound me when the paperwork for the week is late," I said with a hand on my hip.

"Oh, you'll have plenty of time to finish that." She walked out in front of us. "Let me just tell Tasha to hold my calls and cancel my afternoon."

As soon as she was out of earshot, I whispered, "And you over here like this is a good idea, why are you trying to get out of here so bad?"

Nic looked at me with her eyes narrowed and said, "I don't know why you aren't." She shrugged. "You know Mama Mercy will open that wallet and pour out a blessing," she joked. She started toward the door. "Besides, you know I hate shopping for dresses, so I might as well get it over with."

I looked at Liv, who shrugged and followed behind Nic.

On our ride to Sur, Mama turned the music down and asked, "Who will be accompanying you to the gala?" She looked to me first, sitting in the passenger seat, trying to avoid her questioning stare.

"Joseph," I said softly. She smiled in return, and I thought she'd move on to the backseat where Nic and Liv were sitting— unbothered by the game of twenty questions.

"Are you two getting serious?" I didn't have a straight answer for her, because we had recently reconnected, and to claim we were serious after a break seemed disingenuous. But to end the line of questioning, I wagged my head. "I see. There will be a handful of eligible bachelors at the gala, maybe you can switch him out." She tapped the steering wheel as if her mind was churning, before she proclaimed, "I'm sure someone will be a perfect match for you." Before I could defend my relationship with Joseph, let her know he was a perfect match, or demand she stop trying to hook me up, she had already moved on to my sisters.

"You know, Mama, our generation of women is not trying to race down the aisle like you all were when you and Daddy got married," Liv said matter-of-factly. I turned to watch their interaction. "It's perfectly okay to not be paired with someone."

"Hmm," my mama scoffed. "Go on through life thinking you are Ms. Independent till all you have left in your pool of eligible bachelors will be divorced men with kids."

Liv didn't reply, she just sighed and shook her head. "Well, I wouldn't mind a baby daddy," Nic chimed in through the silence. "I won't have to go through the pain of pregnancy, the kids can come over, but their mama won't let them stay too long." She laughed. "Sounds like a decent arrangement to me." But she couldn't just leave it at that, she had to lean forward and say, "I don't know why you didn't think so."

We were parked in front of the strip of boutiques, and all eyes were on me. "What is she talking about?" my mama asked as she stared at me over her oversized sunglasses.

"I met a guy, and he was getting a divorce, had a couple of kids," I blurted. "But I wasn't with it." With that, I opened the car door and stepped out. My sisters stepped out next, and my mother made her exit dramatic—taking her time to exit, as we waited curbside watching her clutch her purse, shake out her shoulder-length curls, and take deliberate steps in her six-inch heels.

She walked into the nearest boutique and commanded the attention of the nearest sales clerk. "We will need a few rooms, and a variety of gowns." She looked at each of us. "Preferably darker colors." The sales clerk elicited the help of her colleague and gathered up what seemed to be their entire collection of dresses. My mother, of course, already had options for the gala, so instead of joining us in the dressing room, she browsed the store until we were ready to begin modeling our options.

"That, my dear, is gorgeous," she said to me as I stepped out in a floor-length, burgundy, chiffon dress with a lace bodice. I twirled around and smiled, until she boasted, "I can't wait till we are doing this with your wedding dress." I sighed and made my way back into the dressing room. We each took turns modeling the different dresses until we were each fitted in a dress that matched our bodies and styles accordingly.

"I don't know about you..." Nic looked at each of us as we left the boutique. "But shopping sure does make me hungry." She rubbed her stomach for extra effect. Mama Mercy shook her head and popped her trunk before she agreed, "If you are hungry, dear, we'll go up the street and grab a late lunch." She emphasized late, and then guilted us by asking, "It may make for a late evening for you all, no?"

Nic had no shame when she replied, "Actually, I think we should be fine." She looked to Liv. "Right?" Liv shrugged her shoulders.

It was I who decided to break up the little party. "I, on the other hand, have a ton of work to finish up." It didn't matter, though, because Nic and Liv convinced our mother that the rest of the night would feel even worse if they didn't stop to eat.

As they walked in front of us to find a restaurant, Mama Mercy looked at me and softly said, "All work and no play, you remind me of someone I know." She winked then added, "But if you take nothing else from me, remember that you need balance. Maybe when we get back to Rolling Hills you can head home early, call up your friend, and grab drinks."

I cocked my head at her because she wasn't the one to de-prioritize work, ever. "You feeling okay?" She nodded her head gently, but it wasn't believable. "You would tell me if you weren't, right?" I asked as Liv and Nic opened the door to a cafe.

"Yes, dear, I am feeling fine." She emphasized 'I,' and I immediately assumed there was something wrong with my dad. But before I could ask, we were being directed to our table and I didn't want to alarm my sisters before I had details.

The last time we were with them for Sunday dinner, he seemed fine. Moving around like usual, chatting us up with all his side banter like he normally would. I watched my mom from across the table, and maybe I imagined it, but her face was holding a few extra worry lines, and although she laughed at Nic's inappropriate jokes, it looked like she was hiding something.

As we pulled into the parking lot of Mercy Beauty, I asked her, "What are you and Dad doing tonight?" She shook her head and told me they didn't have plans. "I think I'm going to stop by to see Dad." She reached across the console and touched my knee.

"I'm sure he'd like that."

As soon as I walked through their oversized front door, I yelled, "Dad."

To which he replied, "Who is yelling in my house like they lost their damn mind?" as he walked down the steps dressed in a jogger set and tennis shoes. Looking as fresh as he did when he was in the league and traveling to away games.

"Hey, Daddy," I said as I opened my arms to wrap them around him.

"Your mama didn't tell me you were dropping in." I looked up at him, and he added, "But I'm glad you're here."

I snuggled in a little closer before I stepped apart and said, "Figured I'd drop in on you since I hardly see you around Mercy Beauty anymore." He laughed and walked toward the kitchen where he asked what my drink choice was for the evening. "What are you drinking?" I replied.

He took a deep breath before grabbing a glass and responding, "Crystal clear water." My dad was a connoisseur of expensive liquor, drinking at least a glass or two each evening.

"Water?" I repeated back with a cocked head. "You feeling okay?" I didn't let him know Mama Mercy already teased something was wrong.

"Your mother can't hold water." He took a long sip. "I'm fine. Now what do you want to drink? Or did you just come over here to be nosey?" His tone shifted from nurturing to annoyance.

"She didn't tell me anything," I corrected him, "she just seemed a little off today." I laughed. "We had a mid-day shopping trip to Sur, and sat down and enjoyed lunch."

"What's wrong with that? You know your mama loves to spend money." He poured white wine into a glass he was holding and passed it to me.

"In the middle of a workday?" His eyes grew wide. "Exactly." My mother loved to spend money, but I didn't know if she loved it more than making money.

"It's nothing serious, really. Doc just needs to run another test on my prostate."

"Nothing serious?" My mouth dropped. "As far as I know, repeat prostate tests weren't a thing, so what's really going on?"

He shook his head. "Too early to know. I'm not worried." He looked to the front of the house. "But your mama seems to be freaking out a bit."

"As she should," I mumbled after taking a sip of my wine. "So, until then"—I looked at his half-filled glass of water—"you kicking your liquor to the curb?"

He shrugged. "Your mama thinks I can eat and drink healthy and all will be well." He smirked. "Let's go outside."

I followed him outside to his favorite set of seats overlooking the expansive land behind their house. "Tell me what's going on with you though." He took a sip of his water, almost as if his glass was full of his favorite bourbon.

"Not much, really."

I continued looking out into the manicured yard until he asked, "Right, and that man you brought over here, how does he feel about that?" I laughed because my dad had never been one to be subtle. Direct was the only way he interacted with anyone, including us. "I mean, if you ask me, he was better than that other guy you brought around here, Lenard, Kyle, Daniel, whatever his name was."

I turned in my seat to look at him attempt to find Calvin's name. "Daddy, you know his name." He shrugged. "But I also think that Joseph is better for me than Calvin."

"I'm not going to argue about that." As much as Calvin tried, my dad gave Calvin a hard time, all the time. "Something about Kevin just rubbed me the wrong way." He smoothed his hand across his beard, fully gray but thick. "Maybe because that time he asked me if I could get him tickets to the game."

I sighed, because despite my pleas for Calvin not to ask my dad, he did it anyway. "Yeah, I don't see Joseph ever doing something like that."

"What do you see him doing?" My dad asked, leaning forward, taking another sip of his water.

I grinned. "I see him accompanying me to the gala next weekend."

My dad didn't return the smile, in fact, I may have seen him grimace. He adored the foundation, and especially the work we did for underprivileged young men, but the "hotsy totsy" stuff we did like the gala and fundraiser balls, he was not into at all. "Is he looking forward to that?" I looked up into the air and he added, "Who am I kidding, he looks like he'd enjoy it as much as I do." He paused. "Not at all." I heard the door open, but my dad kept speaking. "Then after that, what's next for the two of you?"

"Are we talking about my favorite topic?" my mother said over my shoulder.

My dad looked back to her and said, "And what would that be? Spending money?" He laughed as she gently tapped his shoulder. "We were just talking about this guy who may be better for her than that other guy, Daniel."

My mom repeated, "Daniel?" then looked to me. I shook my head.

"We were talking about the gala actually, and how excited Daddy was to dress up in his tux and accompany you. Greet all the people who are donating their time and efforts to the foundation, founded in *his* name." I smiled at him and his nose flared.

"I know that's a lie," my mother said before telling us, "I have some dinner ready, if you want to join us."

I stood from my seat and tapped my belly. "But of course I want to join you."

My daddy mumbled, "Better learn how to cook so you can make that man a good meal."

My mother's neck rolled around faster than I could respond, and said, "Or he better know how to find his way around a kitchen."

My dad scoffed, and I laughed at the both of them as we made our way back into the house.

CHAPTER TWENTY-TWO

JOSEPH

When I entered the lobby of the hotel and saw the sign, "Mercy Family Foundation," I smiled and looked down at my favorite Mercy family member. She was looking back up at me and said, "Are you ready for this?" with a smirk.

I nodded my head, and followed her up the stairs to the event space. Marcia tried to warn me that the gala was way over the top —drinks flowing, fancy food, important people—but I didn't realize it until we stepped inside. We were in Rolling Hills, but it didn't feel like we were in Rolling Hills. I wiped my hand across my beard as I looked around the room, meticulously decorated with the foundation's colors—green and blue, the colors of her father's last football team. There were waiters, dressed in tuxedos or black dresses, walking around with silver trays and small plates.

But I found the one with a tray of champagne and snagged a glass for Marcia and myself. "Thank you," she whispered as she continued guiding us through the event. "My sisters should be around here." She looked around the room. "There they are." She beelined straight toward them, and as they traded niceties, I smiled and hugged each of them, complimenting them on their attire. Marcia's sisters were both beautiful, and dressed for the gala, they were even more so. I diverted my eyes as they started talking about one of the attendees across the room.

Instead of listening in to them gossip, I searched the room for my mama and saw her standing across the room with her boyfriend. His bowtie matching the dress I helped her find at the boutique, perfectly. I shook my head and took a sip from my glass —then coughed as I watched his hand glide across her ass when they walked toward the dance floor. "Hell naw," I mumbled under my breath.

"What's wrong?" Marcia's hand was on my forearm. "You okay?"

I was still watching my mom like a hawk when I responded, "I'm good."

She stepped in front of me and waited for me to make eye contact with her. "Would you like to dance so you can have a better view to watch her?" She raised her brow.

I couldn't tell if she was joking or not, but I took her up on her offer. "Actually, yes, would you like to dance?" I asked, taking her glass of champagne and placing both of them on the table near her sisters. "We'll be back," I said to the two of them before taking her hand and leading her to the floor. Marcia and I had never danced, not formally. But I was glad for the dance lessons my mother made me take as a teen, because the dance floor looked like a scene off *Dancing with the Stars*.

"Mr. Long." Marcia looked up to me as we glided across the floor, me leading the way. "I didn't know you could dance." She grinned, and I shrugged.

"There's so much more you still have to learn about me." She nodded her head. As the song ended, we were beside my mom and Marcia nodded toward her. When she stepped to my mom's boyfriend, I took the shot to grab my mom's hand and lead her during the next song. "You look amazing tonight," I whispered to her as she smiled widely.

"And you remembered your dance lessons." She winked. "I'm glad I made you go, even though you'd fuss all the way there and all the way home." I didn't respond, because it was true. I was the only kid in high school who had to rush home for ballroom lessons. My dad tried to convince me being light on my feet would help on the court, but I'm not sure how much it did, or not. But it kept my homeboys from riding me about going. "And Marcia looks stunning."

I looked toward where she was on the other side of the dance floor and agreed, "She does."

"The two of you make a lovely couple." Her eyes had this look, I didn't know what it was but when she finally said, "I think you may have found her," I knew her mind was not on the night, but maybe a little into the future.

"Found her?" I repeated naively.

My mom rolled her eyes. "Don't play dumb. You know what I mean." Both of us laughed, and as the song came to an end she thanked me, "Thank you for the dance, Jojo." As Marcia made her way by my side, she warned, "But make sure you are worried about the right lady tonight, okay?" I nodded my head. Before I walked away, I reached my hand out to shake Reggie's hand.

"Looking sharp, Joseph." He nodded his head in that old man approval way. I nodded mine in return.

"Better now?" Marcia asked as we left the dance floor.

I replied, "Thank you for the dance, Ms. Mercy." Her cheeks blushed.

The rest of the night was filled with speeches from notable Rolling Hills residents—including our mayor, and a few of the mentees I knew from the gym. Then to cap off the night, they held a silent auction, to which Marcia convinced me I needed an art piece for my living room. But as it was held in the air for display, her sister Nic mumbled, "Put that old African art in your house if you want to, be haunted by all types of ancestors on the regular." She looked at me with her eyes wide. "I'd go for something less...negro spiritual." I laughed as she looked around the room. "Grab some game day passes." I looked to Marcia, who was just rolling her eyes.

I pointed to Nic and said, "That's probably a good idea." Although the football stadium was a few hours away, game day passes would make it well worth the drive. I stood from the table to put in my bid for the passes, and left Marcia with her sisters. "I'll be right back," I whispered in her ear before I walked away.

As I was folding up my bid, I heard, "I'm glad you made it, Joseph." I smiled as I turned to see Mr. Mercy himself. "You know..." He looked down at the game day passes on display. "I could have gotten you those for free." He arched his brows.

"But isn't this for a good cause?" I asked. He shrugged and we both laughed. Marcia had already shared that her dad wasn't into these galas. "I think those little dudes deserve it, right?" I knew he was all for mentoring the youth. He'd made several appearances at the gym to talk to them, and from what I heard he was deeply involved in the foundation—mentoring guys of all ages.

"Ah, guess you're right." He put a hand to my shoulder. Then he turned to look out around the room. "Are you enjoying yourself?" He took a sip from his glass and I noticed the liquid was crystal clear. When I met him at their house he was sipping on whiskey, and I remembered Marcia saying he collected whiskey. The thought of him not drinking it at the event where it was likely flowing was a little odd.

I explained that having my mom and his daughter in the same room, dancing and eating good food, was as close to, "Perfection," as I could imagine it.

"A family man." He nodded his head. "I could sense that about you." He looked across the room to where his daughters sat around a table. "Just wait until that expands to children." He placed his hand over his chest. "Then you'll really know what life is all about." He shook his head slightly then announced, "I better go mingle a bit more before my wife gets on to me."

He turned to walk away and as he did, I looked over to the table again and saw a guy—his face hidden—standing near Marcia. Maybe he was a co-worker, or a member of the foundation. I walked across the room and as I got closer, the guy didn't budge from his position near Marcia, his hand on her arm. I looked over at Nic, then to Liv, who both had their eyes dead set on their sister and didn't notice me approaching.

"Everything okay?" I asked as I stood beside the table, behind Marcia.

The guy looked up to me and nodded his head. "Yeah, we're good man. Don't need anything else to drink."

I cocked my head, and as I did, Nic looked to me with her eyes bulging. Before she could say anything, Marcia shifted in her seat before standing beside me. "Boris, this is my boyfriend, Joseph." We hadn't used titles, yet, and I had to admit, hearing her say it did something to me.

But that feeling fleeted when the guy across from us repeated, "Boyfriend?" and sounded deflected.

I reached my hand out for him to shake, but he just looked at it in disgust before he turned to walk away. I looked down at Marcia when he was out of sight and asked, "He good?"

She looked from me to her sisters, and back to me before she responded, "That's the guy." Apparently I missed something, because that description alone did nothing for me. I stared at her and waited for her to elaborate. "You don't remember him from the restaurant?" I narrowed my eyes then turned to find him in the room, with no luck.

"The guy you were dating?" I rubbed my beard. "What's he doing here?"

"I'd imagine someone on the planning committee did their due diligence with reaching out to professionals in the surrounding area." Her explanation was a P.C. answer, but I needed the non-corporate response.

"Okay, but was he over here"—I pointed to the table—"trying to talk to you? I assume he thought he still had room to slide in?"

I heard one of her sister's make a noise, but my eyes didn't leave Marcia's.

"He wasn't here long before you walked up, and he was asking for a dance."

"A dance." I nodded my head. "Got it."

When I didn't say anything else, she snaked her arm around mine and said, "Before you swooped in, I was going to tell him all my dances are reserved for you."

"Yeah, I noticed you introduced me as your *boyfriend*."

With a blank face, she responded, "Are you not?"

I grabbed the lapel of my tuxedo and straightened my back. "You're damn right I am." Then I heard a whistle from her sisters and turned to wink at them. "And since you were saving all your dances for me, I should use them up." I led us to the dance floor, and we slid across it to a few songs before the band announced the night was over.

"You know, this is the first time I stayed until the end of the gala." Marcia looked around us, the room half empty. "Thank you." She reached up and kissed my lips, and not a sweet, we are in public little kiss either. One that had her tongue all down my throat. Had me almost forgetting we were in public, with her family likely in near sight.

Her hands cupped my face, and she said, "We should get out of here so I can have more of that." She grinned.

Before we could make it to the exit, Mrs. Mercy herself intercepted us. "Looks like you two had an exquisite evening." She looked between the two of us before reaching up to Marcia's face.

"A little lipstick smeared." She grinned at me. "Headed home?" she asked with a smirk.

"Yes ma'am, I'll get her home safe and sound." She looked up at me and nodded slowly.

"I would expect nothing less." She stood aside and added, "Be careful with your dress, darling, remember to unzip it first," she whispered to Marcia, but loud enough for me to hear.

"Wow," I said as we made it out of the hotel lobby. "I didn't expect that."

Marcia just shook her head and said, "Get me home, babe, before I have to ignore her advice and rip this dress off."

I got her home quickly, because ignoring Mrs. Mercy was the last thing I needed to do.

CHAPTER TWENTY-THREE

Marcia

"Chris, of all his friends?" Nic was following closely behind me complaining about Chris being at the barbecue Joseph and I had planned. "Christopher Baxter?" she repeated again, as if I needed to hear his full name for some reason.

"Nic, shit, what do you want me to do now?" I asked as I set a plate on the table.

"Ask that man to find some more friends. To dig deep. Someone he can call real quick." She sighed. "I thought this was supposed to be some sort of matchmaking shindig." Nic truly looked distraught. Like bent all the way out of shape.

"I mean, there will be others," I said nonchalantly. We had already discussed having an equal distribution of women to men, and Joseph had to invite homeboys from out of town to fill his quota. "They just don't live here full time."

Nic groaned. "So if I hit it off with one of them, I'm going to have to catch flights?" She shook her head. "Where is Liv?"

Because neither my house nor Joseph's would be big enough to entertain more than a few friends, and we didn't wanted to inconvenience Mrs. Long, we had to ask Liv to open up her home. She gladly agreed, but warned, "If any of these folks have bad energy, I may stop them at the door."

"She's around here saging or something." I looked over Nic's shoulder. She wasn't the only one looking for our youngest sister. I could use her to run interference between Nic and me—Nic was on my last nerve and I was trying not to snap on her. "Are you finished with the fruit tray?" I asked as I laid the last plate down on the table.

"Yes, and why are you setting the table for a barbecue anyway?"

"Oh my goodness," I finally said as I exhaled, "You need to go find something to do." I cut my eyes at her. "And fast."

She rolled her eyes in response but walked away. And as she disappeared, Liv appeared seemingly out of nowhere with a spray bottle. "And that's the type of energy I didn't want all up in my space." She lifted the bottle and sprayed the air. "If she weren't my sister, she would have been denied entry."

I just looked at her. "Between the two of you, I don't know what to do right now."

She pointed toward the edge of her yard where Joseph was standing over the grill. "You could go help your man pull the chicken off the grill." She grinned.

"If that was supposed to have some sort of romantic connection, I missed it." I looked at her with my head cocked. She just shrugged and walked away, spraying the outside air with each step she took.

I stood back and looked at the two tables we had set in Liv's backyard. Although it was a barbecue, and outdoors, I still wanted it to have an elevated feel. I was pleased with the look— the floral centerpieces, the silver chargers with white plates, and folded napkins.

I heard someone say, "I bet they are going to surprise us with a wedding back here." I turned around with my face scrunched. "I mean, look at it." It was Daysia, my assistant, talking to her good friend, Jayla. When she saw me looking at her, she acted as if she wasn't just talking about me. "Oh, hey, girl."

She reached her arms out and wrapped them around my neck. "Thank you for coming." I looked down at my watch and added, "You are a little early." I tipped my head in her direction. "You aren't ever early, for anything."

Jayla smiled and reached her hand out for me to shake. "Amazing what motivation the prospect of new men brings about." I smiled, knowingly. "I can't blame her for being excited." She grit her teeth. "Rolling Hills isn't exactly overflowing with eligible men."

I looked back to Joseph, and thought about how lucky I was to meet him, even if it was a setup. "Right." I looked at both of them and asked, "Drinking?" Daysia hesitated slightly. "Here, you are not on the clock, don't worry," I reassured her.

"In that case..." She smiled. "Let me grab something strong." I laughed and left the two of them to find a seat at the table.

I felt a hand on my lower back as I entered the kitchen. "That's the last of it." Joseph stepped around me and opened the stove. "I didn't expect anyone to be on time." He looked at the glasses in my hand. "I was actually going to change real quick." I narrowed my eyes as I made my way back to the backyard. "I don't want to smell like smoke all night."

"Right, good idea." I took the glasses out to Daysia and Jayla, but before I could make it back outside, there was a knock at the door. "Liv, you got it?" I yelled out to the ether, not knowing where she was in the house.

"Yeah," she shouted back. I looked toward the front door and she was standing, defensively, with her sage water bottle in hand. I just shook my head and hoped whoever it was had good energy.

"Here you go." I handed them each a glass and let them

know, "Folks are arriving now." I smiled then said, "Make your-self comfortable, I'll bring out some snacks."

I headed back into the house, and realized I'd likely be moving around all night. I looked down at my heels and made an executive decision to ditch those. I had to find a replacement pair of shoes though. I navigated through Liv's house to her closet, thankful we were the same size shoe. I grabbed a pair of her flat sandals and checked myself out in the mirror. "Hey." Joseph looked down at my shoes and laughed. "Heels not working for you?" I shook my head. "Good." He nodded. "You should be comfortable at a barbecue." He winked and leaned down to kiss behind my ear.

"Keep that up and I'll be getting real comfortable at this barbecue," I warned, throwing a look at my sister's boho chic bed.

He gasped, "Not in your sister's bed." I cocked my head. "Let's get out of here before I take you up on that offer."

Back outside, a crowd had begun to form, and I smiled as everyone had already started to mingle. My sisters were among the crowd chatting it up with the guys and the ladies. "Hey," I said as I sat down a platter of dip, pita bread, and the fruit tray Liv pulled together. "I'm glad you all could make it." I looked to the guys, none I had met before, and smiled. "How about everyone introduce themselves?"

Joseph stood beside me with a glass of liquor in his hand. "How about we do the introductions." He moved a hand to the lower side of my back. "We got my right-hand man, Alonzo, right here looking all dapper in the all white." Alonzo was ready for his shout out and wiped his shoulder down. Joseph called out each of his friends, ending with, "And all the way from the ATL, we have my man, Derek." Derek waved a hand in the air, and as he did, I watched Nic's grin grow wide.

It was my turn, and I tried to match Joseph's energy, intro-ducing each of my homegirls with enthusiasm. "To the beauty, who helps me more than she knows, Daysia." Daysia stood from her seat and greeted the group of us with a pageant wave. Each person after, including my sisters, smiled wide and waved as I introduced them—and suddenly I felt like we were on a dating show. "Alright, we have food, drinks, and after we eat, if the guys want to get beat in a game, we have a few decks of cards."

Everyone spread out, starting little pods of conversations, and Joseph and I went between each before I announced, "Alright, if we can all find a seat, we'll start bringing the food out." I made eye contact with Joseph, and he followed me into the kitchen.

"Out here being the hostess with the mostest," he said as he followed behind me. "Think any of them will hook up?" Joseph wasn't up for the matchmaking idea I had initially, but I guess the thought was growing on him as everyone mingled. I arched my brow. "I mean, why not, right? We hook a couple up and maybe we'll have years of good sex."

The platter of mac and cheese I was carrying almost crashed to the floor as I started laughing uncontrollably. "The logic?"

"Good karma, baby," he said without skipping a beat. "Don't drop that mac and cheese," he warned. "I haven't had a chance to taste it yet." He helped me balance my platter and the dish of chicken he was carrying. "You good?"

I laughed again. "Yeah, I'm good."

We joined the group at the table, sitting beside each other, after we had all the food placed. I watched nervously as a few people started taking their first bites. "I used all of Mama Long's recipes." But it was definitely a labor of love, one I was about to give up on and call in an order at a nearby restaurant instead. But when I heard someone say, "Okay, Jo and Marcia doing the damn thing in the kitchen." I sighed and sat back, taking a bite myself.

I felt Joseph's hand on my thigh. "I'm going to have to tell my mama you did your thang with her mac and cheese recipe." He didn't stop to hear my response; instead, he shoveled another fork full of food into his mouth.

Daysia offered to help me clear the tables, and as we were wrapping up, a game of spades started at one of the tables. "I'm so happy for you, Marcia." Daysia was standing near the kitchen island as I rinsed off a plate.

I turned around and asked, "What are you talking about?"

She looked toward the door. "All of this love, your cooking, that man." She grinned. "This shit is inspiring." I couldn't help but laugh, although the look on her face was serious.

"Any of the guys catch your attention?" I turned back to the dishes in the sink.

"How about all of them?" I heard her pout. "It's like a chocolate wonderland out there." She laughed along with me. "I'm serious, though, Joseph came through."

I thought back to my earlier conversation with Nic, and wondered if she felt better with the full lineup of guys at the barbecue. "Well, maybe, just maybe, you'll hit it off with one of them." Then I remembered Joseph's comment about karma, and hoped she did hit it off with someone, hell, anyone. "Better get back out there before they are all scooped up." I smiled over my shoulder.

"You're right," she said before she scooted out the back door.

I was putting the last dish in the dishwasher when I heard an uproar of laughter. I dried my hands and hurried outside to see everyone up dancing and laughing. I found Joseph and, without saying a word, maneuvered myself in front of him. "Be careful how close you get," he whispered in my ear, "I may have to steal you away from all our friends."

"Don't threaten me with a good time," I said as I turned to face him, wrapping my arms around his neck.

"I love you, Marcia." His eyes lowered and he leaned in to kiss my lips. The music faded away, the people surrounding us felt as if they had disappeared, my hips were swaying, and my heart was fluttering. When he pulled apart, my lips remained slightly opened, and I was about to repeat the words he said to me for the first time when he winked and shook his head. "Tell me later."

I didn't want to wait until later, but the noise crowded in and one of his homeboys was beside him asking, "You ready to wrap up this game of spades?" I looked beside us to the table, cards still set out.

"Only if you are ready to get your ass whooped," he responded with a kiss to my forehead before leaving me standing in the middle of the yard.

"You know how long he's staying in town?" Nic stood beside me with a glass of wine in her hand. I looked at her and narrowed my eyes. She nodded toward Joseph and his homeboys. "Derek, all the way from the ATL," she said with enthusiasm.

"I thought I saw you get a little excited when Joseph introduced him." She shrugged. "But I assume he's here for the weekend." I hunched my shoulders like she did.

"I may just have to catch flights and feelings." Then she rolled her eyes. "But I can't even pull him aside for longer than a second without Chris giving me a death stare." I looked over to Chris, who happened to be sitting beside Derek.

I smirked. "Sounds like you have a little dilemma there."

"Hey," Liv said, standing in front of us. "Has Mama tried to call you two?" I looked at her and shook my head because my phone was likely in the house and I hadn't checked it all night.

Nic replied, "I don't even know where my phone is right now." Then she cocked her head. "Why, what's wrong?"

"I don't know." She looked at her phone before putting it to her ear. "She called like three times."

My heart sank. I hadn't even told the two of them about my visit to my parents' house and my dad's health scare.

I couldn't hear what my mom was saying on the other side of the phone, but from the look on Liv's face, it had to be serious. "Okay, we're on our way." Liv looked at the two of us then to the crowd of people in her backyard. "It's Dad, we need to go to the hospital."

I walked over to Joseph and whispered in his ear, "We have to leave, my dad is in the hospital." He hopped up from the table and nodded his head. "Wait." I put my hand to his chest. "Can you make sure everyone gets out okay?" He looked around and nodded again.

"I'll meet you there."

CHAPTER TWENTY-FOUR

JOSEPH

Rolling Hills General was my least favorite place in the world. When my mom called me to tell me my dad's health was failing, I rushed home and spent countless days and nights near his bedside.

With Marcia's dad being in the hospital, it was like an eerie déjà vu. But despite how I felt, I knew how tough those days were for me, and I wanted to be there for her.

When I told the crew what happened, they all piled into cars and followed me to the hospital. "Has he been sick?" Derek asked me from across the waiting room.

"I don't think so." I thought back to the gala and how he wasn't drinking liquor. "Last time I saw him he looked like he was in good health." Then I thought back to seeing my dad for the last time, in seemingly good health, and remembered how the doctor said had he known sooner about his diagnosis, maybe the outcome would have been different.

I stood from my seat and began pacing the floor. Since arriving at the hospital, we hadn't seen Marcia or her sisters. Despite me calling, I still didn't have an update. I appreciated my homeboys and Marcia's girls being there, but it had been a couple of hours so I announced, "I'll let them know you all were here, but—" And before I could finish, Marcia walked into the waiting room.

I rushed up to her and she wrapped her arms around my neck. "They aren't sure what happened, yet," she said to me before looking around the waiting room. "You brought them all here?" she asked with a thin smile.

"No." Daysia stood beside her. "We insisted on coming." She reached out and rubbed Marcia's back. "How's Papa Mercy?"

Marcia took a deep breath before responding, her voice shaking when she said, "They aren't sure."

My eyes narrowed. "What made him come to the emergency room?"

She looked up to me then to everyone in the room. "He," she hesitated, "had blood in his stool."

My eyes widened. "And was he sick before this?"

She wagged her head. "I think so." I didn't know if she lacked information or was being intentionally vague. I didn't pry any more in case she didn't want to divulge all the details.

"Okay." I looked around the room and said, "I was just about to tell all of them they didn't have to wait around."

She nodded her head. "Right, and thank you for coming, I really appreciate it." She looked up to me. "Maybe you should go home and get some rest too." She looked at her phone. "It's getting late and I'm not sure how long we'll be here for."

I shook my head. "I'll wait." The response surprised me because it was the last place I'd ever want to be, but I remember those days in the hospital waiting on answers, or just sitting aimlessly.

Daysia looked up at me then to Marcia and said, "Call me if you need anything at all." Marcia nodded her head, and most of our friends departed with Daysia.

"I'm going to grab coffee for my mom," Marcia said with a strained voice.

I could get to the coffee station with my eyes closed. "I'll walk with you," I offered, then decided, "Actually, do you want me to just grab it for you?"

She shook her head. "I think I need to walk." I knew that feeling—hopeless, restless, tired.

We walked side-by-side, but didn't exchange any words until we were standing in front of the coffee station, and I asked, "What about your sisters?"

She stared at me blankly before responding, "Yeah, they probably need a cup of coffee too." That was it until we made it back to the waiting room and she tried to insist, again, "You should go home and get some rest. I'll call you when I leave."

I shook my head and repeated, "I'll wait." She smiled softly and walked away.

I sat across from Derek, and as soon as I was comfortable, he said, "You really digging her, aren't you?" He was looking down at his phone most of the time he had been in the waiting room. I didn't realize he had even noticed our exchange or anything that was going on for that matter.

His question didn't need a response, but I nodded my head anyway. "Yeah, and it's weird." I looked at him then looked up the hallway where the nurses were shuffling patients between the waiting room to behind the doors. "We are very different, but somehow we work."

Derek chuckled. "Yeah, I see just how different you two are." He leaned forward and said, "She's nothing like your ex." His eyes widened. "Like, at all." I nodded my head slowly because he was speaking the truth. "What's next?" He rubbed his hand across his expansive beard. "I mean," he continued before I could answer, "when you asked me to fly out here for a barbecue, I just assumed it was because you were about to propose to ol' girl, or announce you got her knocked up." He laughed, too hard. "Like, maybe a surprise gender reveal."

Derek was my guy—we went back to freshmen year in college. Met in the dorms during a Madden competition and had been kicking it ever since. He saw all the chicks throughout those years come and go. With my ex, he wasn't necessarily a fan, saying she seemed like a lost soul. Whatever that meant.

"Damn, man, you had an entire narrative down, didn't you?" I laughed slightly before getting serious. "You know, you're single, a couple of her homegirls are single." I shrugged. "Besides, what else would you have been doing?" He wagged his head. "Did you connect with any of them?"

"I don't know," he mumbled, "you may be on to something with these Mercy girls."

"One of Marcia's sisters?" I shook my head and added, "I take that back, if it's one of the two, I already know."

"Oh, you know me like that, huh?" He shifted in his seat, his elbows resting on his knees. "Which one then?"

"Nic." He wiped his hand across his mouth. "You always have liked women with a little sass."

He quickly added, "And a whole lotta ass." We both laughed.

"Now I know why you were trying to stick around." He pointed to me. "You know, Rolling Hills isn't such a bad place to live."

He shook his head feverishly. "Naw, bruh, I'm going to leave this little ol' city for you." He tapped his leg. "Besides, I'm not even on that right now. I still have some years in me before I'm trying to settle down." He shifted in his seat. "Wait." His eyes narrowed. "Are you trying to become Mr. Mercy?"

I couldn't stop the laugh that was rolling from my mouth. "Bruh, for real?" I laughed more. "Mr. Mercy."

The smirk on his face accompanied with, "You trying to tell

me she doesn't run shit?" had me feeling some type of way. I stopped talking and looked down the hallway again.

It felt like hours had passed since the last time I saw Marcia. The drinks had worn off, my stomach was growling, and Derek had fallen asleep leaned over in the chair. But then I saw Marcia and her sisters emerge from the hallway, and I stood to greet them. "What's going on? Is he going home?" I looked behind them.

Nic was the first to answer, her voice strained, "No, not tonight anyway." She looked to me, then her sisters, before she sighed and walked over to where Derek was still sleeping.

Liv smiled softly. "Maybe something good came of this night." She looked up to me and asked, "Can you get her home?" Then she looked over to Derek and Nic. "I'll get those two where they need to go."

"Of course." I looked down at Marcia, whose makeup had smeared, the pins in her hair had been removed, and her outfit was in shambles. I looked down at her feet and said, "Good thing you changed into those sandals."

Before Liv walked away, she warned, "And I better get them back in good shape." Marcia rolled her eyes.

I reached for Marcia's hand and she wrapped her fingers around mine, gently. As soon as we were settled in the car, she rambled on about all the tests they would have to run on her dad. "I thought they had done most of the tests already though," she said faintly.

"You knew your dad was sick?" I asked.

She didn't respond; instead, she said, "Thank you for staying, I know being in a hospital couldn't have been easy for you." She stopped short of mentioning my dad. "Thinking about it, I don't know what I would do if something happens to him," she admitted. "Watching my mom tonight, powerless, hopeless." She didn't continue, but I knew what she was trying to say. I felt the same way about my mom when we were in the hospital. The thought of them being alone after spending years with someone is difficult to imagine.

When I parked the car, I didn't know if she needed to be alone or if she needed me, so I asked, "Do you want me to stay?"

She looked at me, her eyes glossy, and responded. "Please."

"Say less." I opened my door and walked over to hers, helping her out of the car.

"I just need a shower," she said after setting her purse and keys on the counter.

After a long day, and even longer night, I didn't have much energy left, but the thought of her naked under running water inspired me to ask, "Can I join you?" Her hesitation to respond made me offer, "Just a shower. Nothing more."

"Would it be weird if I wanted more?" Her eyes danced around, looking everywhere but at me.

I knew that feeling. That feeling that all your energy, emotion, time should be dedicated to caring for your person—the one who was sick. Finding that balance between not losing yourself and feeling obligated to give your all to them. I assured her, "If that's what you need right now, it's not weird at all." I pulled her into my arms, and if my words didn't reassure her, my dick certainly did.

Her hand went down to meet it, and she moaned softly before saying, "It's exactly what I need right now."

We didn't hesitate any longer. I led her to the bathroom, started the shower, and stripped her out of her clothes. As she stood there bare, I kissed behind her ear and down her neck. When the shower became steamy, I sent her in alone, at first. Then I followed right behind—taking my place behind her, my hands immediately going to her back and massaging small circles as I saw her head relax forward.

I left no muscle untouched, massaging down from her back to

the heels of her feet. When I was finished, we stood under the stream of water together, her head rested on my chest. "Here," I whispered, "let me lather you up." I grabbed the bottle of soap and squirted it in my hands. She hardly moved as I cleaned every inch of her. "I'll meet you in the bedroom," I told her as I helped her step out of the shower.

I quickly cleaned myself and turned off the shower. I towel dried even quicker and headed to the bedroom before Marcia had a chance to fall asleep. Instead of finding her with her eyes closed, she was sitting up in the bed, her head laid on the pillow, and she looked to be staring at the ceiling. As I got closer to her, she said, "Thank you." I crawled beside her. "For being here."

"You don't have to thank me," I responded. But thank me she did when she straddled my lap and rocked her hips back and forth, her head falling back as she moaned. Neither of us mentioned the slip up, not that night or the next morning when we woke up, our bodies still intertwined without a condom between us.

I slipped out of the bed. I would have cooked us breakfast but when I opened her fridge, there were only bottles of water and condiments. I shook my head and snuck back into the room to grab my clothes. I slipped out to the grocery store to grab a few staples, and expected Marcia to still be sleeping when I returned. "Hey," she said when I walked back in through the door.

My eyes widened, and I said, "Hope you don't mind me taking your keys. I didn't want to wake you when I made it back."

She looked down at the bags and smiled. "It's cool." Then she looked down at her feet before she said, "Maybe it's time I give you a key anyway." She closed the gap between us, placing a hand on my jaw. "There was something I needed to tell you." I cocked my head. She didn't say anything. Instead, her mouth went to mine, and her tongue parted my lips. I let the bags drop to the floor and I wrapped my arms around her waist, pulling her even closer to me.

When she pulled away and looked up to me, her grin was even wider. "What'd you have to tell me?"

"I love you," she said confidently.

I kissed her forehead and said, "And I love you."

CHAPTER TWENTY-FIVE

MARCIA

"You're still here?" My dad looked up from his cup of coffee and frowned.

I had the same sentiments, but I didn't dare tell him I was over being his play nurse as he recovered from his surgery. Because although he was the most difficult patient, I was glad he was home, and on the road to recovery. "Be careful, old man, last time I checked, you kinda needed me to bring you your food," I joked.

He waved his hand in the air dismissively and responded, "Your mama is doing too much. I told her I can get out of this bed and get it myself." He threw the covers back and swung his feet over the side of the bed.

Thankfully, he did not have cancer, but he had some serious polyps that had to be removed from his colon. The doctor told him to take it easy for at least two weeks, and we were approaching day ten. I placed my hand on his arm. "She's just downstairs," I warned. He groaned before he put his feet back into the bed. "I didn't think you wanted that smoke."

My mom had been home the entire time my dad's been out of

the hospital, and when he was in the hospital she never left his side. But my sisters and I had been cycling through their house to help her take care of him. More so me than my sisters, who claimed they couldn't handle my dad's attitude.

"How is Mercy Beauty operating if the operations manager is over here playing Nurse Betty?"

I rolled my eyes and shook my head. I pointed to the corner of his room where I had my laptop plugged into the wall. "When Nurse Betty gives her patient his pills and he goes off into dreamland, I am able to get some things done."

"And what about your boyfriend, if you are over here every day, where's he at?" That was a question I couldn't answer as easily. I bit my lip. "See, you over here worried about me, and your man left you." He flung the covers off of himself again. "Tell your mama I'm fine." His feet hit the ground and before he could stand, he warned, "Stand in my way and I'll plow you over like we were on the field."

"Dang, Daddy," I laughed, "it's like that?" I watched as he slowly made his way toward the bathroom. He wasn't as imbalanced as he had been days earlier, and he was moving around with ease. "I'm good." He waved his hand in the air. "Go find your man."

I collected my makeshift office and stuffed it all into my bag and headed down the stairs while my dad was still in the bathroom. Before I could even reach her, my mom was up on her feet headed toward me. "What's going on?" she asked in a panic. "Why do you have all your stuff?" She looked down at her watch.

"Dad told me to tell you he's fine." Her eyes opened wide. "He's in the bathroom now, and I watched him walk over from the bed." I hunched my shoulders. "He seems to be okay." When she didn't move or respond, I asked, "Are you okay?" I crossed my arms across my chest.

Her shoulders slumped, and she said, "That man is insuffer-able when he isn't well."

I nodded my head and with a slight smile, I agreed. "For all of our sanity, I hope he is better." She laughed and opened her arms wide, and I walked into them with ease. "He told me I need to go take care of my own man."

She giggled in my ear before she whispered, "At least he still has his sense of humor." She pulled away from me and said, "He has a point, though, you've been over here almost every day for a few weeks now." She narrowed her eyes. "I hope you've at least spoken with Joseph." And my eyes diverted away from hers. "Marci," she gasped.

"I know." I cringed. "I know." She pointed toward the door, and I took her direction. "Love you," I shouted over my shoulder.

I didn't wait till I made it to my place. Instead, I called Joseph from the car, and as soon as I heard his voice—raspy, deep, sexy— I turned my car in the direction of his place. "Are you home?" I asked.

When he said, "No, actually, I'm not." I looked up at the red light and waited for him to elaborate, but he didn't.

"Okay," I finally said. Then I admitted, "I was hoping I could stop by."

"I won't be home for a while." Before I could say any more, he asked, "Can I call you back?"

"Yeah." I tapped on the steering wheel as I made the U-turn back to my place. "Of course."

I pulled into the parking garage, grabbed all my bags, and made my way to my door. As soon as I walked inside, I dropped my bags and called both Liv and Nic. "Hey," I said when Nic answered, "I'm adding Liv in too."

When they were both on the phone, Nic grumbled, "Oh shit. What happened?"

Liv quickly asked, "Is it Dad?"

Not realizing the call to both of them could alert them, I reassured them, "No, not Dad. He's good, actually."

"Thank God, I don't know how you spent so many days over there," Nic went on mumbling. "He'll mess around and end up with a permanent spot in a nursing home fucking with me."

"Damn," Liv and I said in unison. "That's cruel," Liv shouted.

The two of them continued bickering until I interrupted. "I was calling to talk about Joseph."

"We need to ride out?" Nic responded before I explained the situation.

"It's weird," I said slowly. "I just got off the phone with him, and it's like he didn't want to talk to me."

"Oh," Liv said softly, "When is the last time you saw him?" I paused because I couldn't remember what day it was, or how recent. "That long?"

Nic interrupted, "I wouldn't have time for your ass either."

Liv responded with more empathy when she said, "But Daddy was just sick. Of course, he knows what that is like."

She tried to defend me, but Nic wasn't having it. She calmly replied, "And that's maybe more so why he doesn't get how you could ghost him." That shut up Liv and me. "You were at least talking to him during this time, right?" When I didn't respond, she groaned, "Marcia, what the hell?"

I snapped, "I've been busy. With work, and at their house when I'm not at work, hell, most days working from their house." I didn't realize tears had started to stream down my face until I sniffled.

"Are you crying? Marcia, for real?" Nic's voice was softer. "Maybe he was just busy." Then she warned me, "Don't go find another man in the meantime." We all laughed.

Liv offered, "Yeah, I'd say he was just busy and he'll call you back and all will be well." I hoped they were right, and that night

I waited for him to prove them right, but hours had gone by and he hadn't.

It wasn't until I laid my head down on my pillow that I heard my phone vibrating on my nightstand. "Hello?" I tried to answer like I was fully awake, but I wasn't.

"Did I wake you?" he asked. I just laughed instead of trying to convince him I was wide awake. "Your head wrapped in your flower scarf already?"

"It is." He tried to tell me he'd call back in the morning, but I wanted to hear his voice. I wanted to know what happened earlier when it felt like he was blowing me off. So instead of letting him get off the phone, I said, "Were you busy earlier?"

Like he had no idea what I was referencing, he said, "Ugh, when you called?"

"Yes," I simply replied. His long pause was unexpected. "I feel like there is something you need to tell me."

"Can I be honest?" I felt my heart leap into my throat. I sat up in my bed and braced myself for the next words that would come from his mouth. "I was in my feelings." My eyes narrowed as I listened to him explain, "When my dad was sick and I came home to help my mom, the one thing I wished is that I could have someone alongside me that I could lean on when things were getting really bad." I tried to interrupt, but he continued, "When you told me he was in the hospital, I was prepared to be there with you for as long as he was there."

"Joseph," I finally said, "I was thinking that would be too much to ask of you, especially after all you had been through."

He laughed. "Guess that's why they say people should over-communicate."

I admitted, "Whoever they is, is likely right." I nodded my head, although he couldn't see me, and said, "Lesson learned." He went on to ask about my dad and when I told him he was doing much better, I said, "I miss you."

"Is that right?" I confirmed, and he asked, "How much?"

"Enough to pull off this scarf and drive across town to see you." My hand was already moving toward my head, and I was throwing the covers back, hoping he'd say I could do just that.

Instead, he said, "You stay put. I'm on my way."

CHAPTER TWENTY-SIX

JOSEPH

My hand hovered over the mouse pad as I watched Marcia pace the floor. "What good is the head of operations if the business can't operate without you?" I probed. Things had been going good between Marcia and me, real good. Her dad was doing much better, and if the two of us weren't together, we were at work. The thought of a little get-a-way came up when I was scrolling through my phone and saw the Arizona spa on my screen. Initially, Marcia was thrilled with the idea of a 'baecation,' as she called it, then she later told me that she needed to check her schedule.

I let her 'check her schedule' for a week before I told her, "If we don't book this trip, we'll never go."

"Besides..." I put my laptop beside me and pulled her arm as she was walking past me. "When is the last time you even left Rolling Hills?"

She looked at me and shrugged. "When I was in college, I imagined I'd be spending these years, you know, before marriage, traveling the world with my sisters, or my homegirls."

"Or a boo," I interjected, and she cocked her head before

laughing. "No? You didn't imagine having a sexy ass man laying up beside you in bed, windows open as you listen to the waves?"

She put her finger to her chin. "Actually, no." I laughed before she explained, "Maybe it was because I didn't see that with any of the guys I was dating in college. I didn't see beyond what we had then."

I nodded my head. "Fair."

Then she interjected, "And laid up listening to the ocean." She narrowed her eyes. "What ocean will we be listening to in Arizona?"

I raised my free hand and waved it through the air. "It was a hypothetical." We both laughed, and I pulled her into my lap. "Mama Mercy will be okay without her dearest daughter for a few days."

"You're right." She kissed my lips. "Book it." I scooted her off my lap, and she yelped as she plopped onto the couch. "Damn, babe."

"I'm just saying, I need to book this trip before you change your mind or something."

Good thing I did book the trip, because for the weeks leading up to it, she wavered on her decision, trying to convince me the time wasn't right, or that she had meetings that couldn't take place without her. Even as we sat on the airplane beside each other, I had to pry her phone from her hand when I saw she had her Mercy Beauty email on the screen. "Yo, what fun will this be if you spend it thinking about work?"

She grinned and pulled her phone back. "I was turning on my out-of-office message." I watched as she closed the email app and opened her music app. Then she pulled out her headphones and handed one to me. "For the remainder of this flight, you can call me DJ Bae."

My eyes grew wide, and I couldn't help but laugh at the nickname she had given herself. It didn't matter, though, I was just glad she decided to take the trip with me and seemed to be loosening up.

Her DJ skills, though, a few times I had to shake my head and tell the DJ to flip the song. "I have love for the female rappers, but Marcia, for real? It's not a hot girl summer for me."

She started laughing and changed the song. "How about I give you this?" And when I heard the smooth track, I nodded.

"That's what I'm talking about." I leaned over the armrest and kissed her earlobe. "Get us to Arizona in the mood." Our eyes connected. "Thankfully, this flight isn't too long."

Her hand went to my inner thigh. "And that's why I was trying to keep the songs upbeat." She licked her lips. "The flight may be quick, but not quick enough." She shifted in her seat and rested her head on my shoulder.

I vaguely heard the flight attendant announce our descent into Phoenix, but I sat up as the plane hit the runway and I felt Marcia's hand clench my thigh. "You okay?"

She nodded. "Yeah, I must have fallen asleep." We grabbed our bags and headed for the exit. "Carefree, Arizona," she repeated as we climbed into our rental car.

We were headed to a resort spa, in Carefree, Arizona, and had a thirty-minute ride through the desert. "Have you been to the desert before?" she asked as her eyes stayed plastered on the passenger window.

"No, this is a first," I said as I watched the barren land we passed. "I'm not sure how I feel about all this dirt." I laughed. "Give me some lush green grass, and some oxygen-producing trees."

She started laughing uncontrollably. "Yeah, I was just sitting here wondering why we didn't go for the ocean view."

"Damn Facebook ads. They'll sell ice to a damn Eskimo."

"Facebook made me buy it, one helluva drug." We laughed and pointed out different sites as we continued to the resort. "I will say that the mountains are breathtaking though." I had to agree.

The lobby was full of people, men and women, who looked well rested. I walked to the check-in desk, and as I confirmed our stay I noticed Marcia was no longer by my side. Instead, she was standing in front of the lobby windows gazing out. "Don't worry, many of our guests get caught up in that view." The woman behind the desk reassured me. "If there is anything you need to make your stay more pleasurable, please let us know." She handed me the room keys and said, "Be well," as I walked toward Marcia.

"Ready to go up to the room?" I asked, but when she didn't budge my eyes followed her gaze, and I was equally mesmerized. The drive to the resort—the dry land and lack of greenery—was less than desirable. But the view of the mountains and the well-placed cacti served as a backdrop to the endless pool, and it was, "Breathtaking."

"I know." Marcia looked up to me. "I think this is exactly what I needed."

She reached for my hand and we walked to the elevators. "It'll be hard to return home after this."

She grinned wide. "Isn't it always hard to return home after vacation though?" I shrugged. "If only I could find a way to forever be on vacation."

I knew, if Marcia had the courage, she would quit her job and be doing something else. "What do you think it'd take for you to make that a reality?" The elevator doors opened, and I thought my question was lost, but as we walked into the room, she responded, "To be honest?" I nodded my head. "Forever vacation would be a stretch because obviously I'd need to make money." I wagged my head. "But I've been thinking about a life I don't need to vacation from, one that's less stressful, and enjoyable."

"Is your life not enjoyable now?" I followed her to the window with a similar view to the massive mountain.

"Enjoyable, yes. Stressful, definitely." She hunched her shoulders then sat on the couch near the window. "It's just not what I would have expected to be doing at this point in my life."

We had talked about it before, so it was no surprise to me that she wasn't happy working with her family. I didn't want her to dwell on it, so I changed the topic. "Until we become independently wealthy, we have to enjoy the vacations." I smiled. "Do you want to sit out by the pool?"

Her face grew into a wide grin and she hopped up, walking over to her suitcase. "Just wait till you see my bathing suit." My eyes grew wide and I could only imagine what she was going to put on—her curves fully dressed left little to the imagination.

When she came out of the bathroom I had already changed into my trunks and a tank, and was looking down at my feet to put on some slides when she slipped in front of me. "What do you think?" She spun around, and the gold bathing suit shimmered against her deep-brown skin.

I told her, "Wait," as her back was turned to me, "All of that?" I said as I admired her ass. "And you expect me to want to leave the room?" I huffed. "Naw, I don't see that happening." I stood and grabbed her by the waist, pulling her into my chest.

I kissed a trail from her ear down to her chest. "Keep that up and we definitely won't be leaving this room at all."

"Is that supposed to be a threat?" I asked as I spun her around. She giggled as I pulled her up by the waist, wrapping her legs around me. "As a matter of fact." I backed her up against the wall. "My idea of a perfect life is this right here." My lips landed on hers and I kissed her until I heard her moan. With the mountains as our backdrop, I slid her bathing suit to the side and entered her slowly.

"We should," she said between moans, "use a condom." She

was right, we had already flirted with danger enough. I placed her to the ground and ran over to my pants laying on the bed. The condom was on and I was back to her before she could change positions.

I kissed the smirk off her face as I wrapped her legs back around me. There was no corner of the room too sacred for us. I carried her from the window, to the couch, and finally, we landed on the bed. When I laid her down to climb on top, she shook her head. "Let me." I laid down and she straddled my waist.

There wasn't a thing in the world that Marcia Mercy didn't do with her whole heart—including riding my dick. She did that without abandon, with passion, with love. She confirmed it when she leaned down and whispered, "I love you," into my ear as she slowed down her pace. I heard her hiss and moan before she kissed me alongside my jaw.

I was trying hard to hold out, but when she bit my bottom lip, I lost it. I grabbed her by the waist and cautioned, "Hold on." I took a long breath then said, "I'm about to—" But she didn't let me finish. She leaned down and swallowed my words—and my tongue. Her hips went back to rocking—back and forth—and it didn't take long before I was done.

"We keep this up, the only sight we will see will be these four walls," she said as she slipped beside me. "Although, I'm not sure I'd be mad about it."

I laughed and cupped her chin. "I need to figure out how vacation Marcia can stick around more." I kissed one cheek. "No offense to working Marcia, but this one right here..." I kissed the other cheek. "Has her beat."

She tapped my chest then sat up on the bed. "Let's go by the pool." I wanted to just lay there, but the look of excitement on her face made me sit up too. I pulled a shirt over my head and was ready to go, but she disappeared.

"Okay, ready," she announced when she returned from the

bathroom. An oversized hat, glasses, and long see-thru shirt added the Marcia touch to her golden bathing suit.

"I don't know if I should walk beside you or behind you and capture pictures," I said as I walked toward the door.

"Just make sure you catch my angles," she answered with a straight face, and I just shook my head.

I wasn't prepared for hours sitting poolside—no books, magazines, or an iPad full of content. Unlike Marcia, who had a bag full of entertainment options. "I was just thinking we'd drink Mai Tais and hop in the pool when it got too hot," I responded when she asked why I didn't have anything.

"I have this book." She tried to hand me a book on entrepreneurship, and I frowned. "No?" I shook my head adamantly. She put all her options down and made her way to my reclined chair. "How about..." She leaned in closer and pulled her hat down to the side, blocking our faces from the crowd before she kissed me slowly. "We take a dip in the pool?"

"I was hoping I could have more of those lips." I rubbed my arms that had sweat in places I didn't even realize could sweat. "But a dip in the pool sounds like a good option right now."

She laughed and wiped a hand across my forehead. "Yeah, this desert heat is no joke."

Although Marcia's hair was braided, I expected her dip in the pool to include a few toes splashing in the water. So when she walked down the stairs of the pool and swam a lap to the other side, my mouth dropped. On her return, she asked, "What? You thought I couldn't swim?"

I blinked my eyes a few times then said, "I just assumed you wouldn't want to get your hair wet."

She threw her wet braids over her shoulder and said, "Babe, that's why I am rocking braids. It's vacation." She smiled. "I'm indulging in everything." That comment alone had me wanting to pick her up and carry her back to the room but instead, she splashed my face and asked, "You can swim, right?" I smirked then dipped into the cool water and took a lap of my own. "Okay, I see you, black man."

We continued splashing around the pool until she told me she was hungry, and we returned to our lounge chairs and ordered lunch—poolside. "I swear," she started after chewing a bite of her sandwich, "I could live like this all the time." I nodded as I chewed a French fry. Then her eyes grew wide, and she said, "Oh my goodness."

I looked over my shoulder, expecting to see something crazy the way she shouted. "What?" I asked nervously when she wasn't speaking.

"I got it." My eyes narrowed and I waited. "Mercy Beauty & Wellness needs a spa." Our eyes connected, and hers were lit with excitement, mine not so much. I was about to remind her that we were on vacation and Mercy Beauty was not supposed to be top of mind. But then she added, "Rolling Hills needs a spa— and we should open it."

I coughed on my French fry, because I thought, "We, as in you and me?"

She cocked her head then clarified, "Well, not you and me, we, but Mercy Beauty." I nodded my head. "That's my exit plan. That's my vacation every day plan."

She was too excited for me to burst her bubble. To let her know that opening a completely new line of business would not only feel like work, but a hell of a lot of work. "Exit plan," I repeated. "But not one you'll think about now." I looked down to her plate. "Hurry and finish your food, we have more to explore." I licked my lips, hoping she was picking up what I was putting down.

Her hand reached over and massaged my thigh, and I knew she had.

CHAPTER TWENTY-SEVEN

Marcia

Before walking into her office, I paced the floor a few times. "I got this. I can do it," I repeated to myself softly. I closed my eyes and whispered, "Dear God, let this go well." Then I held my shoulders back, my head high, and I walked into my mama's office.

Mid-day visits were rare, Mama Mercy stayed busy. Even though I was her daughter, I had to go through her secretary to get on her calendar. "Hey, dear," she said as she looked up from her computer screen.

Her makeup was flawless, she looked like she had a good eight hours of sleep, her hair was perfectly curled—Mama Mercy was the epitome of Mercy Beauty and Wellness. She embodied what she preached to women of the world.

"Have a seat." Her eyes narrowed. "Are you okay?"

I took a deep breath to compose myself before I replied, "Yes, I'm amazing actually."

She grinned. "I bet." She winked. "Fresh off of vacation with your boyfriend." I nodded my head. "You'll have to catch me up on that later." She looked out of her door. "Tasha told me you wanted to discuss a business opportunity?" She grabbed a notepad and a pen. "I'm listening."

"The vacation actually spurred the business idea." She sat back in her seat. "We should open a spa." The idea rolled off my tongue and bounced off of the wall, the silence that followed it was unexpected. Somehow, I expected my mom to be bursting with joy and praise for my idea.

When she responded, "Oh?" I was a little concerned she hadn't heard me, so I repeated myself. "I heard you, dear."

"What do you think?" I clasped my hands together in my lap to keep from fidgeting. The space between my question and her reply felt like an eternity. She wrote a few things down on her notepad, then sat back staring at me, blankly.

"Marcia, our products are manufactured and distributed." She paused. "Internationally." I was very well aware of the stats. "We don't have a storefront." She spoke as if I didn't know that either. "And to my knowledge, we don't have the expertise, in house, to open a spa." Then she laughed. "Unless, of course, you were thinking you'd be in charge."

My eyes widened. "All these years you've told us what steps to take to be successful. How to maneuver college, our career." I laughed. "Even my love life." I unclasped my hands and sat up straighter in my chair. "Not once have you taught us how to be creative. To forge our own path. To navigate our own dreams." Her face fell into a frown. "I don't blame you." I looked around her office. "What you've built here is already successful, we just had to step into the roles you had for us and be happy."

"Marcia," she tried to interrupt me.

"I don't know about Olivia and Nicolette, but I'm not happy here."

Mama Mercy stood from her desk and circled around to the front. Her hand was on my back when she said, "I'm not sure if I agree with your characterization of me." She sat in the seat beside me, with a hand outstretched to my knee. "I've encouraged all three of you to create a career that will be fulfilling."

"Here." Our eyes connected. "You've encouraged us to stay here."

I saw the hurt in her eyes when she replied, "Maybe I'm naive, but I thought your dream was to be here." I shook my head. "And had this conversation went differently—had I said okay to your spa idea, you would feel more fulfilled?"

I thought about her question. "Honestly, probably not." She moved her hand from my knee and asked what I was looking for in my life. "Independence. The opportunity to create a balanced life."

She simply said, "Do that."

"Tasha will have my resignation letter. I'll take two weeks to help find my replacement."

She bit her lip. "I didn't mean for you to quit, dear."

"But to *do that*, I don't have any other choice."

She slowly blinked then agreed, "Maybe you're right. Regardless of your employment status here at Mercy Beauty, you'll always be my baby. If I can help in any way, I'm here."

"Thank you, Mama." We stood and embraced before the door opened and Tasha informed us that my mom's next meeting was starting shortly. "I'll see you later."

I walked back to my desk and closed the door behind me. My body was buzzing. The last time I remembered feeling that, alive, was when I first started dating Joseph. Then I sat down and fell back against my chair. "I just quit my job," I whispered to the universe. "And I have no backup plan." I unlocked my computer and logged into my bank account. "Shit," I whispered. My account balance informed me that I'd probably need a plan expeditiously. Then my computer chimed with a notification—team meeting. I'd also have to make sure they were prepared to handle the department when I left.

My team gathered around me at the conference table, and I contemplated informing them of my departure in two weeks. Before the meeting kicked off, I decided it was best they knew what was going on—I was practicing full transparency. "I'm glad you're back," Daysia said with a wide grin, "I can't wait to hear about your trip." She looked over at my hand, and her nose scrunched. I narrowed my eyes at her, but her face returned to a grin.

"I had a great trip." I looked around the table making eye contact with each of my team members. Over the years, my team had grown from Daysia to a team of five. Five amazing men and women, who gave more of themselves than I ever asked. "In fact..." I paused and took a deep breath. "I submitted my resignation today."

Gasps spread around the table, but it was Alex, my right-hand man, who spoke up first. "What do you mean you submitted your resignation?" He shook his head. "You're leaving?" he asked with concern.

I nodded my head and responded, "Yes, in two weeks." His eyes widened. "But don't worry, I'm going to make sure you all are ready to take over in my absence."

Although I tried to maintain eye contact, everyone had diverted their gaze away from me. Then Daysia said, "Not to be all in your business, but," and she proceeded to be all in my business when she added, "where are you going?"

I laughed and replied, "I'll let you know when I have more details." I smiled. I opened my laptop and said, "Until then, I better get you all ready. Let me hear what happened while I was out." They proceeded with a narrative, describing all the issues, things to work on, and new deadlines that just by listening already had me overwhelmed.

I walked out of the conference room ready to head home—or to Mrs. Long's house for dinner—but Daysia caught up with me, tapping me on the shoulder. "Ma'am," she said in her fake southern accent, "that may have been a good enough explanation for them, the folks who have worked with you only for a couple of years." Then she pointed to herself and said, "But we've worked together longer than that. I'm your assistant," she emphasized with her eyebrows raised.

I shook my head. "Honestly, I wish there was more to share. All I can say is, I want to venture out a bit, and Mama Mercy wasn't feeling the idea." Her mouth hung open. "It's okay, though, this was probably best."

"Alright, I'm scheduling time on your calendar to talk more about this," she warned. "Get out of here, I know you have dinner tonight." I nodded my head and appreciated she always had my calendar memorized. She leaned in for a hug. "Just for the record, I will probably miss you the most." Then she lowered her voice. "But if you think I'm sticking around here to be Alex's assistant, we have to talk about this." I laughed. I knew she and Alex had a contentious relationship. She felt that Alex was always overstepping his role. I couldn't say I disagreed, but I tried to maintain a positive outlook.

I stuffed my laptop into my bag, because after dinner I'd definitely have to start working on my exit strategy and a business plan. I hurried out of the door before anyone else could stop me, and drove across town to the address Joseph texted me earlier. I grabbed the bottle of wine from my passenger seat and walked up to the door. But as I waited, I realized I didn't see Joseph's car in the driveway.

I had started to dig for my phone when the front door opened. "Marcia, come on in, girl." Mrs. Long's boyfriend, Reggie, was standing in the doorway wearing a wide grin.

"Hey," I said calmly before walking into the house behind him. "Uhm, I didn't see Joseph's car outside."

"He had a little emergency come up with work." He looked

at me then frowned. "Surprised he didn't tell you." He shrugged. "Anyway, he should be here soon." He fanned his hand through the air. "You can come join us in the kitchen."

Maybe Joseph did try to warn me, but I didn't want to be rude and pull out my phone. I held up the bottle of wine to Mrs. Long and said, "Can I put it in the fridge?" She nodded her head. "How are you?" I asked after I dropped my purse in a seat. "Do you need any help?"

She laughed. "I'm doing well, Marcia." Her hand was moving quickly across the chopping board. "Just finishing up these peppers for the stew."

Reggie was walking around the kitchen aimlessly. "I should set the table." He looked at Mrs. Long and she nodded.

As Mrs. Long described the stew she was cooking, I looked around the kitchen and imagined Joseph there as a kid. Then I saw a picture of him standing with a girl on the kitchen counter. I assumed it was his sister, who I had yet to meet. "Is that Tanya?" I asked.

By the smile that spread across Mrs. Long's face, then quickly faded into a frown, I knew that was her. "I'm starting to think she doesn't know how to get back home." I knew his sister was in Tokyo for business and I assumed she came home to visit. But when Mrs. Long said, "You'd think after a year you'd miss your mama." She shook her head. "Nope, I don't know who raised her," she joked.

A stream of air carrying the scent of the stew went past my nose, and I said, "If she hasn't returned for her mama's cooking, at least, then she must be really enjoying herself."

"Or enjoying that man more than missing her mama." My eyes widened. "I don't know about this generation of women." She picked up the chopping board and scraped the peppers into the pot. "You'll let a man change your whole life plans." I started coughing, patting my chest, hoping it'd subside and when it didn't, she went to the fridge and grabbed a bottle of water, handing it to me while she patted my back. "You okay?" I nodded my head and was relieved when I heard the front door open.

"Is that you in here coughing up a lung?" Joseph said as he stood back and watched his mother and I interact. "I'll be right back." He held up a bag. "I need to change."

Mrs. Long moved back to the stove, stirring the contents. "I let her know," she continued, as if I hadn't just had a whole coughing fit, "whoever she's tangled up with, he is welcome to come for a visit too." She continued on about how women these days always had to be around their guy. "You all act independent." She smacked her lips. "But it makes me wonder sometimes."

Joseph walked in and said, "You wonder what?" He wrapped his arms around my shoulders and kissed my cheek. His arms felt like home, and I suddenly realized it was probably a man that kept his sister from visiting. Because although she may have missed her brother, and especially her mama, strong arms could feel like home too.

Joseph walked over to his mama and gave her a kiss to her cheek before he slapped hands with Reggie. "Good to see you, man." Reggie had a cool smile on his face when he heard that. "Need any help?" he asked, walking over to the stove and peering into the pot. He looked back at me and said, "Did my mama tell you I love this stew?"

I laughed. "She didn't have to, you've been raving about it for weeks." He winked.

There was no help to offer, because the stew was ready, as Mrs. Long said, "We were just waiting for you to show up, honey, the food is ready." Reggie and Joseph both cheered. "Marcia, baby, grab the cornbread muffins, will you?"

Grabbing the cornbread muffins was the least I could do, but I did it with a grin and a nod. As we sat around the table, Joseph looked to Reggie and said, "Go ahead and bless the food, Reggie." I didn't know if it was a test of his holiness or just Joseph being kind. Whatever it was, Reggie's prayer was a little long winded, and I had to pop one eye open to see if we were still praying moments later. "Amen," Joseph cleared his throat then said, "Maybe I'll do the prayer next time." We all laughed.

Joseph had every right to hail his mama's stew as the best meal he ever had, because it was delicious. But when she offered, "I can give this recipe to you too, you know?" I cringed.

"Mrs. Long, I'm not sure I do your recipes any justice to be honest," I said, which caused her to go into her spiel about *women today.* "I've survived this long without really cooking." Why did I say that?

"And you've been single most of those years?" I sensed a little sarcasm in her voice, but I just nodded my head. "Maybe that's why, baby?" I looked to Joseph with my eyes wide.

"Mama," he said defensively, "a woman's worth isn't in the kitchen," which seemed to shut her up, and somehow made my panties wet. I placed my hand on his knee and smiled gently.

I was thankful it was the middle of the week and I had an excuse to exit Mrs. Long's house shortly after we had coffee and cake. Joseph walked me to the car and said, "Hey, I apologize." His face looked strained. "My mama can be rude at times."

I laughed and shook my head. "I mean, maybe she has a point. Maybe that's why I have been single all these years." Joseph pulled me into his arms and snuggled into my neck. "The way you and Reggie leaped for joy when the food was ready, people say a way to a man's heart is through his belly." I sighed when he didn't respond.

I started to pull away from his embrace when he said, "Hey, we all love to eat. Obviously, that's what sustains us, and if we have to eat, it might as well be good. Right?" I nodded my head. "But what good am I if I rely on you to feed me?"

I wagged my head. "I guess." Then I placed my hand to his chest and mumbled. "What if I told you I don't cook, and in two weeks I'll also be jobless?"

His eyes widened and his mouth dropped open. "What?"

I looked him in the eyes and proudly announced, "I submitted my resignation today." I expected him to tell me I was crazy, or being too spontaneous.

Instead, he put a hand to my face and said, "I'm happy for you." Then his smile grew wider and he said, "Vacation every day." I nodded my head and repeated it. "I can't wait to hear about your plans." He pulled me closer into his chest then told me, "Let me go thank my mama," then he paused, "can I come over to your place?"

"Absolutely." He kissed my forehead and I climbed into my car.

CHAPTER TWENTY-EIGHT

JOSEPH

The everyday vacation Marcia was different from the working for the family business Marcia. For the first week she'd call mid-day and stop by the office with lunch, at night she'd have some meal she'd prepared from watching cooking shows all day. By the end of the second week, though, she seemed to be in panic mode, saying things like, "I can't believe I quit my job." She'd even look at me and ask, "And why did you let me do that?" As if I had any choice in the situation.

A few weeks in, though, she had settled into her decision, and even started working on a business plan. That was the Marcia I was most excited to see, the one who believed in herself and her dreams. In fact, there were a few nights when I had to slide her laptop to the side and show her just how much of a fucking turn on her drive was to me.

Then came the, "Oh, you're a plumber, you probably have connections Marcia." That one involved a whole lot of me, and wasn't as sexy.

Unfortunately, that's the Marcia that stuck around for a while. I was walking through the gutted building where she decided *Everyday Vacation* would reside, when she said, "I think I need to find someone who can build this stone wall." She was standing in front of an empty space looking from floor to ceiling. "I think it would be a perfect focal point for the entry." She turned to me and smiled. "You know how I got lost in Arizona at the window when we checked in?"

I narrowed my eyes and responded, "Yeah," nonchalantly.

She laughed and wrapped her hand around my arm. "I know this isn't what you signed up for." Her nose scrunched up. "But I appreciate you being here every step of the way."

"Him?" I heard from across the room. "What about us?" Nic stood from the ground. "Looks to me like he's just walking around while I'm over here putting in work." By work she meant she was flipping through paint swatches.

Marcia dropped my arm and crossed the room. Standing in front of Nic and Liv, she proclaimed, "There are no words for the appreciation I have for the two of you."

"There are drinks," Nic quickly replied. "You can pay us in drinks." We all laughed.

"But really..." She pulled them both into a hug, and I couldn't hear the rest of what she was saying. I turned to the front of the building and stared in amazement at what she was able to accomplish in a couple of months. From her vision, that was a little spotty at first, to the building we were occupying.

I knew it hurt her when her mom didn't accept her original idea, but when her dad came through offering to be an angel investor, all else was quickly forgotten.

"Alright, back to work," Marcia said over her shoulder as she walked back toward me. "You sure you don't mind pulling that stuff together for tonight?" I shook my head. "No, I don't mind." Then I joked, "Although, I'm not sure she's going to be excited about the surprise."

Marcia put her finger in front of her mouth. "It's her last year in her twenties, she'll just be happy to celebrate." Marcia had enlisted me in helping to pull together a surprise gathering for Nic's birthday. I was on tap to grab supplies—balloons, flowers, and cupcakes. "Don't kill me," she said, and I already knew she was about to add to my list of shit to do for her sister. I cocked my head. "I know, I know," and she didn't say anything else.

"Marcia, what do you need?" I sighed as the grin returned to her face.

"I forgot to grab her gift from the boutique."

Considering it was just a few doors down, I didn't mind adding that to my list. But I warned, "Okay, I'm leaving before you add anything else." I shouted to her sisters, "See you later." They both waved and continued looking through the swatches.

"Hey," I said when I stepped into the boutique. "I'm picking up a gift order from Marcia."

The clerk's eyes lit up. "Oh, yes, just a second." She disappeared to the back of the store and returned with a pre-wrapped gift box. "I went ahead and wrapped it for her." Her face grew into a wide smile. "I know she's been busy with the spa." I nodded my head and grabbed my wallet from my pocket. "Oh, no, she already paid."

It was my turn to smile. "Great, thanks for wrapping it. That was thoughtful and I'll be sure to let her know." I started to walk toward the front door when I doubled back. "Hey, I just had a thought." I looked around the store, one of Marcia's favorite boutiques. "Marcia hasn't been in lately, well, other than this gift, right?"

She shook her head. "That's how I knew she was super busy." She laughed. Busy or on the brink of being broke, but I didn't tell that to the clerk.

"Yeah, real busy," I repeated. "Let me grab something you think she'd like."

She burst into a fit of laughter. "Really?" Her hand

went to her chest, and I already knew my bank account would hate me for that move. "Right over here." She grabbed the hanger of a nearby dress. "This is her size, actually." She looked at the dress and back to me. "I noticed her eyeing it when she came in, but she insisted she was too busy to try it on." She put her finger in the air. "I will warn you, though, she typically tries on all her clothes." Her eyes widened.

"Okay," I said slowly. "And it's her size?" I asked simply. She wagged her head. I didn't understand how it could be her size and still not fit, but I'd worry about that later. "I'll grab it." Then I asked, "She can return it if it doesn't fit, right?"

She gritted her teeth then said, "Not usually." And I understood why she had to try on every item. "But I think we can make an exception for Marcia." That's the least they could do, the woman shopped there religiously.

She rang me up and sent me on my way, with not just the one gift, but two. I didn't have a plan for giving Marcia the dress, but I had to finish running errands, so I ignored that.

I was headed to the flower shop when my phone rang. "What's up?" I asked, and before he could answer, I said, "You here yet?"

Derek confirmed, "I'm grabbing my bag now." Derek and Nic had been talking back and forth since his visit, and when I told him about her birthday surprise, he was game for a return trip. "You outside?" he asked, and I hesitated before he laughed and said, "Damn, bruh, your hospitality ranking is a zero out of ten, do not recommend." Then he reminded me that his last visit I essentially left him while I camped out in the hospital waiting room.

"Listen, grab a ride to my place, I'll shoot you over the money for your inconvenience and I'll be there..." I coughed. "Soon." Derek started to complain, then I said, "For real."

"Fuck around and you'll have me calling Nic." We both laughed then hung up so I could continue on my boo mission.

Flowers, balloons, cupcakes, and gift in hand, I walked into my place and damn near wanted to pass out from all the errands. But Derek was amped when he saw me, until he realized I was the party. "You planned this party?" he asked, standing with his head cocked as I juggled all the shit in my hands.

I unloaded everything into the kitchen and I explained, "No, but Marcia didn't have time to grab everything, and she's with Nic, so getting away would have been tough." His eyes widened as he nodded his head.

"I don't know if I'm ready for that couple life." I pulled my head back before he continued, "All that honey-do shit, naw, I don't know if I got it in me." I couldn't even refute his claim. I just shrugged my shoulders. "So what you thinking?" He returned to his seat on the couch where he was likely tuned into Sports Center. "You going to make this thing forever?"

He was the first person who asked me that legitimately. Although I had been thinking about it non-stop, I lied and said, "I don't know yet." My relationship with Marcia was solid, but the thought of proposing and getting married was starting to scare me. The last time I thought I was ready for that next step, my entire relationship blew up, and I found out she was cheating.

"Something about that answer sounds like a lie." He turned from me back to Sports Center. "But I'll let you have it."

"I'm hungry as hell, let's go eat."

Derek, with his six-foot, two-hundred-pound frame, hopped off the couch and clapped his hands. "Now we are talking." He laughed. "You're trying to improve your host rating." He shimmied his shoulders. "I see you."

"I would take you over to the bar, but that's too close to Marcia's place, and I can't risk Nic seeing you." I paused to think about the next best place. "There's this lunch spot nearby, but they don't serve liquor." Derek frowned. "I know, but it should be flowing freely tonight."

"Bet. I'll make up for it then." He slapped a hand to my shoulder. "And don't be offended when I don't make it back to your place." He winked. "I already promised Nic the next time I saw her, I wanted her legs wrapped around me and my face buried deep in her breasts."

I cocked my head and quickly said, "Bruh," I shook my head, "I don't even think I needed to know all that."

Then he asked, "But is your homeboy Chris going to be there?" I wagged my head. "I don't want any problems."

I narrowed my eyes. "I think he has a girl now, actually." I already knew Chris was feeling Nic hard, but Nic wasn't giving him any love, at all. "If not, though, I think he's not sweating Nic anymore."

Derek twisted his lips. "Not from what I heard." My eyes widened. "Dude damn near be outside her window with the jukebox in the rain, singing ninety's R&B."

I opened my mouth wide and let out the loudest laugh. "What?" I asked when I finally caught my breath. Derek laughed and just shrugged his shoulders. At the gym, Chris acted like he was completely over Nic. "Let me find out dude lying to save his pride." I shook my head as we climbed into my car.

"Whatever it is, I'm just here for the weekend." He turned to look out the window.

"Not you sounding disappointed." I laughed. "What happened to the you too fly to not be single vibe you've had all these years."

"Even the flyest playas have to settle down sometime." He wiped his hand across his bare chin.

If Derek was considering settling down, then I knew I wasn't crazy for thinking that Marcia might be the one.

CHAPTER TWENTY-NINE

Marcia

Between quitting my job, starting a business, and being a super girlfriend, I had to go add on top of that sister of the year with the little surprise I was trying to throw for Nic. Thankfully, Joseph was beyond a super boyfriend and he deserved some type of Man of the Year award for the shit I was putting him up to over the last few months.

If it wasn't for him encouraging me to open *Everyday Vacation*, I may have still been showing up to Mercy Beauty bitter on the daily, and upset that I wasn't fulfilling my own dreams.

When the fear and the doubt appeared, too often, he'd remind me that the plan would work itself out. As I sat on Liv's couch waiting for her and Nic to finish getting dressed, I thought about how much my love for Joseph had grown. He went from being that guy I wasn't so sure about to that guy I wasn't sure I could live without. My eyes widened as I let that thought sink in. "Oh shit," I whispered to myself.

"Oh shit, what?" Liv asked as she bounced into her living room wearing a long, flowy dress, with her hair adorned with a flower crown.

Before responding to her, I had to acknowledge her hippie get up. "Ma'am, are you going to Coachella?" She laughed and gave me a twirl. "I'm not even mad, you're rocking it for sure."

She grinned and then she looked over her shoulder. "Did something go wrong with the"—she held up air quotes—"planning committee?"

Daysia and Jayla were at my place decorating and preparing it for us all to arrive. "No, not that I know of." I looked down at my phone just in case though.

"Okay, so what's the 'oh shit' about then?" She moved to her makeshift bar and grabbed a martini glass, but filled it with champagne. I narrowed my eyes as I watched her.

"I was just sitting here thinking that Joseph may be the one." I expected her to have the same reaction as I did, but she just wagged her head. "That doesn't surprise you?" As I said that, Nic walked into the room looking equally as cute as Liv. Her high-waisted jeans, crop top, and hair falling into her face in luscious curls were totally different from Liv but definitely cute. "Okay, birthday girl," I shouted. "I see you."

She blew me a kiss then asked, "Where's my glass?" Then she side-eyed it and said, "That doesn't look like a martini though."

Liv shook her head and grabbed a matching martini glass. "But what does that matter? As long as you have a drink in your system." She laughed and Nic nodded her head in agreement. "And you came right on time," she looked back to me and announced, "Marcia is about to be a married woman."

Nic gasped, "Not on my birthday, bitch." Her hand went to her chest.

Liv and I laughed because out of the three of us, Nic was the one to make the biggest deal out of her birthday. Maybe there was something to that whole middle-child thing. "Damn. That's not the response I would have expected," I said between laughter.

"I'm just saying." She sipped her champagne from her

martini glass. "Any day but this one."

"And you aren't surprised I'd want to get married?" I asked.

She looked between Liv and me. "Is that a trick question?" I shook my head. "Joseph is probably the best thing that's happened to you, in a minute." She shrugged her shoulders. "Marrying him would be a no brainer."

I watched both of them drink their champagne as we killed time before we left for the party. The more I thought about it, Nic was right. Joseph was one of the best things that had ever happened to me. Then I stopped. "Did he think the same?" I mumbled more to myself than the two of them dancing around the living room.

But Liv replied, "Are you sitting here overthinking?" She plopped down beside me. "Whatever it is..." She handed me a glass, filled to the brim. "Let it flow."

"You're right." I nodded my head and took a sip of the champagne. "I'm letting it flow." She was definitely the one to motivate me in flow—her sage-burning, flower-crown-wearing, meditating ass was always talking about letting it flow. She gave me a side eye, and I promised, "For real. I'm letting it flow." I winked then said, "We should probably get out of here soon."

She nodded and announced to Nic, "Alright, it's time to celebrate." Nic clapped her hands, although she had no idea what we had set up for her.

"And may one of these bars have a fine ass man." She swayed as she drank the last of her champagne. "Or may the drinks be strong enough for me not to care." She laughed. "I just need to be fucked for my last day in my twenties." She cackled and added, "And the first day in my thirties."

We all laughed and danced out of the house, but when Liv started driving toward my house, Nic got a little suspicious. "What bars are on this side of town?" There weren't many, maybe a restaurant or two that served liquor but not a full lounge.

So I covered by saying, "Oh, I just need to run up real quick and change shoes." It sounded like a good enough excuse to go into the house.

Then Liv added on, "And I should use the restroom one more time." We both looked back to her, and Liv said, "You might as well come in with us."

"You better be quick too." She unbuckled her seatbelt. "I told you I have dick on the mind."

As we walked down the hall toward the elevator, I sent a quick text to Daysia to let her know we were coming. I had explained earlier that they should turn the lights out and hide, but I sent a reminder just in case. I had to avoid looking at Nic in the elevator, and made sure I walked fast to the door so she'd be a little behind me.

I opened the door and didn't see anyone. "Okay, she's coming," I whispered to absolutely nobody. I had no idea how they hid that well, but Liv walked through the door and I heard someone stirring. Then Nic walked in and I flipped on the lights and yelled, "Surprise," and everyone came out from their hiding spots and yelled along with me.

Nic jumped and grasped at her heart. "What the fuck?" she asked, looking around the room. "How'd you two pull this off?" The smile on her face was exactly what I needed. I turned around and saw her friends, and Derek, among the crew. I watched as she made eye contact with him, and I already knew she had plans for him. Before she made her way to him, she pulled me and Liv into a tight embrace. "You two are something else."

I shook my head and said, "We had a lot of help." I turned to find Joseph standing close by. "Boyfriend of the year goes to..." I wrapped him in my arms and kissed his cheek. "Thank you."

Nic stood beside me and said, "Yes, thank you, bro-in-law." I looked at her, my eyes blinking, and she laughed before walking off.

Joseph pulled me in close, leaned down and kissed my neck before he asked, "I know Nic can be crazy, but what is she talking about?" He leaned back and looked me in the eyes. I gritted my teeth and shrugged my shoulders. "Not believable at all," he said with a grin.

I didn't ask him how it felt to be referred to as 'bro-in-law,' although I wanted to know if it made his insides as warm and fuzzy as it made mine. Ignoring all of that, I turned to Daysia and asked, "What's on our playlist?"

She didn't reply; instead, she hit play, and the first song up was one of Nic's favorites, "Pretty Girl Rock." As if on cue, she and a couple of her homegirls lined up and started dancing in my living room.

While they danced, I poured a few craft drinks we designed for the night—tequila, her favorite liquor, pomegranate juice, pomegranate seeds, and a lime. She smiled as I handed her a glass. "Oh, we fancy, huh?" I laughed and passed out a few others before taking one for myself.

Liv leaned on the counter beside me and offered, "You know, next year will be my last year in my twenties." She grinned. "I wonder what my big sisters will have planned for me."

I just laughed and took a sip from my glass. Daysia and Jayla were still playing hostess as they passed around finger foods.

Although I was only a year older than Nic, I was feeling like an old lady a few hours into the party and wanted to escape to my bedroom. I walked over to Joseph and whispered into his ear, "Help me with something in my bedroom." He looked up to me and his eyes danced. "C'mon."

He grabbed ahold of my waist and walked behind me into the room. I closed the door behind us and collapsed to the bed. He laid beside me and asked, "You okay, babe?"

I nodded my head without lifting it from the pillow. "Yes, and no." My eyes blinked slowly. "This is the part where I want to kick them out and go to bed, but."

He laughed and added, "But you can't kick your own sister out of the party you surprised her with." I nodded and nuzzled my head into his chest. "They may not notice you disappeared."

Those words were the permission my eyes needed to drift close. They stayed closed until I heard loud knocking on the bedroom door. "What the hell?" I whispered as I sat up. I wiped my face and looked around the room before I climbed out of bed and opened the door. "Hey," I mumbled.

Liv laughed and said, "Your place is clean, I'm headed out." I looked behind her and didn't see anyone.

"Where'd everyone go?" I asked.

"To the bar?" She shrugged. "I think."

"Damn, my bad." She opened her arms and hugged me tight before she walked to the front door. There was someone I expected to see when I looked around my room and into the living room. "Hey, where is Joseph?" I asked before she opened the front door.

"Oh, he went to take the trash out." She grinned. "I'm sure he'll be back."

As she opened the door, her prediction was confirmed. "You leaving?" Joseph asked Liv.

"Yup, she's all yours." She turned and winked at me before walking out of the door past Joseph.

He walked through the door and as he closed it, he pulled me into his arms. "Hmm, I like the sound of that."

"The sound of what?" I placed a hand on his chest.

"All mine." He kissed my neck. "How does that sound to you?" His warm, full lips were on my neck, and everything felt amazing.

I moaned before I responded, "Fucking amazing." He

laughed. "So fucking amazing."

"Oh," he said loudly and pulled away. "I have something for you." It wasn't the way I expected him to propose. I looked around my condo, and thought it could have been in a better place, maybe with friends, and definitely family.

But as he disappeared, I convinced myself that however he did it, I'd no doubt say, "Yes." The grin on my face was so wide it started to hurt.

When he walked in carrying a bag from my favorite boutique, I had to hide my slight disappointment, then I thought the ring could be inside the bag. "What's that?" I asked softly. He pulled a dress from the bag, one I had looked at recently. Although it wasn't a ring, I was pleasantly surprised. "Aw, thank you." I walked over to him and gave him a hug.

I guess my excitement wasn't what he expected, because he asked, "Were you expecting something else?" He looked down at me. "You look a little disappointed."

"Oh." I tried to recover both my face and my response. "No, it's just..." I smiled. "Thank you for thinking of me."

He laughed. "Yeah, you are definitely disappointed."

I sighed. "Okay, truth?" He nodded his head. "I was just thinking maybe you were going to propose." I closed my eyes then said, "But I wasn't expecting that, I don't know if we are even ready for that yet." I kept trying to explain, but the words that followed were smothered with his lips on top of mine.

"Today?" he said after he pulled away from our kiss. "No." Then he held my chin up and added, "One day?" I looked into his eyes. "I hope so."

I released the breath I was holding then wrapped my arms around his waist. Looking up at him, I said, "I hope so too."

The End

EXTRAS

If you'd like to read more about the Mercy Sisters, check out the following:

- Nicolette Mercy - Love Requested
- Olivia Mercy - Love Delivered

If you enjoyed this story, please leave a review on an eBook retailer, and blast me all over social media. Because as an indie author, I thrive off of reviews.

Thank you for the support!

ALSO BY J. NICHOLE

Visit www.notthelastpage.com/books for a full list of books.

ABOUT THE AUTHOR

J. Nichole is an HBCU graduate, a wife, and a Black mama. She is in love with love, especially Black Love.

For more information:
www.NotTheLastPage.com

Milton Keynes UK
Ingram Content Group UK Ltd.
UKHW010650250923
429338UK00001B/94